THE BOOK OF JUDITH

Also by Stuart Hood from Carcanet

Carlino
The Brutal Heart
The Upper Hand

STUART HOOD

The Book of Judith

CARCANET

First published in Great Britain in 1995 by
Carcanet Press Limited
402-406 Corn Exchange Buildings
Manchester M4 3BY

Copyright © 1995 Stuart Hood

The right of Stuart Hood to be identified
as the author of this work has been asserted
by him in accordance with the Copyright,
Designs and Patents Act of 1988.
All rights reserved.

A CIP catalogue record for this book
is available from the British Library.
ISBN 1 85754 186 3

The publisher acknowledges financial assistance
from the Arts Council of England.

Set in 11pt Bembo by Bryan Williamson, Frome
Printed and bound in England by SRP Ltd, Exeter

Then she came to the pillar of the bed, which was at Holofernes' head and took down his fauchion from thence and approached to his bed and took hold of the hair of his head... And she smote him twice upon his neck with all her might and she took away his head from him and tumbled his body down from the bed... and after she went forth and gave Holofernes his head to her maid; and she put it in her bag of meat.... (Judith, Chapter 13)

Warning to the reader:
All history may be fiction but not all fiction is history

In the room there is only the sound of breathing, shallow, regular, broken by occasional hesitations that lengthen into pauses, rests, silences. They bring the nun from her chair near the window to bend down over the bed and listen. Then with a convulsion, a desperate choking, it begins again, faster now, as if the dreamer were running down some road, some defile, that becomes a great pipe – not a pipe – something flexible, coloured, like the inside of a giant gullet that swallows him down into darkness. Then the pace slackens, the breathing falters, is suspended for a few seconds before it finds once more a gentle rhythm broken only by what might be a sob. The nun's hand reaches out to the respirator mask to feed oxygen to the dying man from the tall burnished cylinder. On the oscilloscope the line of light continues to trace the rhythm of the heart's obstinate struggle. The nun leans over again to feel for the flickering pulse on the sleeper's wrist. Then she checks the needle that drips into a vein the liquid that nourishes him, strengthens him for those desperate fugues that leave a pearling of sweat on his brow. Gently, carefully she turns back the sheet which must soon be changed, for it is becoming damp. On his belly she can see the deep scar, like the pit left by a carbuncle, where on some African hillside the bullet entered that should have killed him more than fifty years before. Further down a catheter runs from the small, brownish slug of his sex. Then as she settles the clothes again, she looks down at his familiar face.

All through her childhood and youth, before she took the veil, she saw it on posters, on the walls of classrooms next to the crucifix, in the pages of newspapers and magazines, with its moustache, its receding grey hair, its smile of power; so she knows it well and can judge how the days of illness have sharpened its features, thinned its cheeks, robbed it of authority. How long, she wonders, will he have to fight before they allow him to reach the goal he strives towards? With the comfort of religion, of the holy oil, the blessing and the sign of the cross and the formula promising *indulgentiam plenaram et remissionem omnium peccatorum* while the incense rises to hang on the canopy above the bed with its damp sheets and pillows.

She turns away from the bed and from the complicated tubes and pipes and wires that mechanically maintain the rhythms of life to the shrine in the opposite corner of the room. On a table with an embroidered cloth fringed with ecclesiastical lace there lies a reliquary. Through its fretted silver she can see skin like crinkled leather and above it the yellow of a bone: the arm of Santa Teresa of Avila, which had accompanied the dying man through the Civil War and into the peace. Above it, in a glass case, the blue mantle, draped as if it hung on the wearer's shoulders, is the robe of the country's patron saint – the Madonna of the Pillar brought from its sanctuary to watch over the death bed. The nun kneels before the shrine and, finding her beads, begins to tell them, not in haste, not running them through her fingers heedlessly, automatically, like an ignorant peasant girl, but pausing on each one, thinking the meaning of the words, feeling the familiar rhythm of the Latin. *Nunc et in hora mortis nostrae. Amen.*

That I can imagine, said Fergus to himself, as he lay on his back in the dark of this foreign room where he must wait for a message, a telephone call, to summon him to a rendez-vous, and listened to a different breathing – that of his part-ner, his companion, his (only in the literal sense) fellow-traveller, who lay there unstirring. Her breath came and went almost imperceptibly, so that he had to raise himself on an elbow and lean over her bed to hear its even rhythm. When he lifted the sheet and covered her naked shoulder the rhythm faltered momentarily. Then he lay on his back and stretched his legs out like a knight on a cathedral tomb – what he had heard himself (to his own surprise) describe to that Wise Woman, his analyst, as 'practising being dead' – so that she looked up from her notes and asked why he thought he should have to practise that? To which he had found no ready response and could find none now in this hotel room, where the vague shapes of the furniture were unfamiliar and as difficult to distinguish as they would be in that other room where the great man lay between life and death, suspended there by a conspiracy of doctors and politicians.

Meanwhile from all over the peninsula, from the captains general who ruled the provinces, from the commanders of the Civil Guard, from the bishops and archbishops, the statesmen, the high party functionaries, the organizations of the secret police, intelligence flowed in on the state of the nation, the hopes and fears of its people, the intentions of those who had dared to oppose him, had suffered under him. From these reports a decision would be taken in the innermost councils of state as to when he might be allowed

3

to die: this hard man who had been a great fighter, who had not turned aside from bloodshed, who had been punctilious in his ceremonial devotions but notoriously indifferent to religion – like his own foreign legionaries with their barrackroom motto: no liquor, no women, no priests. But could that have been so? It was hard to believe that these men who could not resist the seduction of danger and of death (who was their mistress and accomplice) were truly monks of war, chaste and sober, practitioners of a kind of ascesis. Did they never in the Moorish towns, which were their strongholds, go down through the narrow alleyways to where the women sat at the curtained doors of their cells with their tattooed brows and their hennaed hands which fluttered an invitation?

So what images, Fergus wondered, ripple up into the dying man's consciousness when the shallow breathing quickens for a few seconds and the eyes flicker to and fro beneath the closed lids? In what centres of his body and what recesses of his memory do they form? Does he feel on his arm, where the intravenous needle enters, the pressure of the white gloved hand of his bride as they walk together from the church between the lines of soberly dressed women and children? He is smiling – his comrades say he always smiles but never laughs. Perhaps a memory of the feel of her skin, of his exploration of her unfamiliar body in their first, virginal embraces. That is, if at thirty-one he was still a virgin; had never at eighteen, say, as a second lieutenant in the 8th Regiment of Foot, gone with his fellows to the discreet closed houses where the women let their scented hair fall over the faces of men and boys who would one day bring to their marriages a peculiar diffidence – for how does one approach sexually a woman one has not bought, who is not by definition shameless? – together with a strong urge to assert their rights, to establish a family, perpetuate a name and lineage by begetting a son. Which he never did – fathering only a daughter after five years of marriage – so that he had to look for a surrogate in a prince of the blood royal. Whom he cherished like his other cadets, volunteers escaping from poverty or conscripts. All of them he had imbued with the ideal of service to the Motherland over which the Virgin watched whose image was stamped on the medal that lay on his breast – not the handmaid of the Lord, *ancilla Domini*, of the nun's prayers but a warrior queen.

Yet Fergus knew – having taken pains to study his subject – that some of those who had been close to the great man said he was at bottom not a believer: an observer of forms, yes, one who demanded the ecclesiastical pomp that had once been the prerogative of the Kings of Spain, but not a believer. There were even those who found his prayer of thanksgiving in the Church of Santa Barbara (patron saint of the artillery whose salvoes saluted his victory) almost blasphemous in its assumption that he had been an instrument in God's hand in conquering his fellow-countrymen. It was not religion – they pointed out – that he had taught the fresh batches of young men and boys who year after year came to the military academy he commanded, with their hopes and aspirations. What they learned was duty and, as he coolly remarked, 'adequate prophylaxis' to render innocuous their sexual adventures. Yes, he had said, yes, youth had influenced him. Youth in which he perhaps invested his love. Chastely. For he was not like his brother, the exhibitionist, the daring trans-Atlantic flyer, who had brought home the 'wife' he picked up in the cabarets of Morocco and then abandoned; he was truly a bridegroom of war. Witness his marriage, constantly postponed as he answered the call to fight in the colonial campaigns that he had made his name. His motto: Love your Motherland. Love sacrifice. From which it was only a little step to the battle cry of the Germans, Austrians, Frenchmen and Latin Americans of his Legion: the oxymoron – Long live death!

5

What had driven the dying man, Fergus mused as the light slowly began to seep through the curtains, was almost certainly an excitement so intense and so sexual that it had drawn him on to confront the chance and hazards of war, the orgasm of death. An excitement of which he himself felt he had been cheated – had even admitted so under the seal of the confession to the Wise Woman when he had consulted her at a time of isolation, of loss of love or (his greatest fear) of the ability to love.

It was unfair, he had explained, as the gasfire in her consulting room whispered and from somewhere across the square there came the sound of a child nimbly, heedlessly practising scales. What was unfair? the Wise Woman asked. He did not answer because the sound of the piano distracted him. So he paused for a few minutes, allowing a silence to build up into which the Wise Woman spoke her ritual words of dismissal. The session was over. But walking back across the heath he rehearsed what he had meant to explain to her. The wartime excitement as the fighters swarmed up from the airfield under the Downs. The tangle of vapour trails overhead as the planes swirled and glinted above his school. The dead cows in a field where the bomb-craters were lined with chalk like huge dew-ponds. The crashed Messerschmidt fighter in the water-meadows beyond the railway-line. The silhouetted charts of enemy planes, or enemy armoured fighting vehicles on the walls of his study. The cadet force exercises which were no mere game but a preparation for battle when the Second Front would at last be opened on the coast that, on a fine day, he thought he could see when he climbed to the top of the Downs among the anti-aircraft guns and the football-playing gun-crews. With luck school would be over before the invasion came and he and his fellow-cadets called up for the adventure they discussed incessantly in dark of the prefects' sleeping quarters – discussed with the same tingling curiosity as they listened to the oldest of them all tell how he had fucked the family maid under the dining-room table and rewarded her with half-a-crown.

From one of the GIs who lay encamped in the woods behind the Downs waiting for D-Day that same boy had obtained a rare prize, which he treasured and cunningly concealed at the risk certainly of a caning and probably of expulsion: a magazine called *Silk Stockings*. For a small fee – a piece of home-made cake, a share of the sweet ration – he was prepared to unveil with the most stringent security precautions the images of which he was guardian and owner: young women who looked out from the pages with a falsely innocent smile, with a pouted kiss, a glance of mute invitation over one shoulder. But what they most displayed were long legs clad in silk stockings held up by suspenders that disappeared into underwear beneath which lay secrets which Fergus in his tortured innocence and masturbatory guilt could only guess at.

These were images he studied briefly, guiltily, in his cubby-hole of a study where posters called for A Second Front Now and proclaimed that the Red Army's Fight is Ours. Beneath them, on a map of Eastern Europe, a line of little flags marked the Russian advance from Stalingrad and red circles ringed the liberated cities: Kursk, Smolensk, Orel. In the school debating society he had proclaimed himself a Communist – a stance the Rector had ironically sanctioned on the grounds that such a rush of blood to the head was forgivable in view of the propaganda everyone (including the BBC) was putting out. Fergus MacIver's adolescent enthusiasm, he reasoned, would be tempered by age and experience; after all, he had himself been tempted by socialism in his youth. So let the boy have his say.

But Fergus had been too late for the war, which had come to an end a week after the draft he commanded humped their kit up the gangway and onto the boat that carried them routinely from Newhaven to Ostend. His mounting excitement had lacked consummation. That was what was unfair.

He may have been the new red-haired second lieutenant whom I saw one morning in April 1945 chivvying ruddy-faced kids with rifles and kitbags into single file at the bottom of the gangway as I stepped down on to the quay with a fellow-officer, after five years of war in which we had both lost our innocence. 'Jesus,' said my companion, 'don't they make you feel old.'

They would have before them the long slow journey in a convoy of trucks through towns where chicanes of rubble choked the streets. In cratered fields dead tanks sank into the wet ground. By the side of the roads burnt-out SP guns rusted with nearby a clump of crosses, British, American, German, on some of which there might be a pious bunch of spring flowers. Their convoy was drawn east towards the thump of the guns, across the Rhine and into the North German plain. But suddenly the guns fell silent and the convoy halted. For them the war was over.

So instead of action, of that testing of the cutting edge of fear and excitement, there would be the anticlimax of military life in the Army of Occupation. Months spent in a limbo where the defeated enemy in worn and ragged uniforms clustered like insects on the running-boards and roofs of slow trains and the victors, as they counted the days to demobilization, looked forward with ambivalence to civvy street and the loss of privilege, of authority and of the liberties war had granted them. So he would drink in the NAAFI clubs where at the bar the old hands reminisced about the Desert, the Battle of the Bulge, the Normandy beaches, the Rhine crossing, raids over Berlin, and the new-comers danced with young women in the blue uniform of the Control Commission. With one of whom, in a bor-rowed jeep, in the summer of 1945 (still a virgin) Fergus drove out across the Lueneberg Heath; a young woman whose Daddy had chambers in Lincoln's Inn: Sarah, tall, blonde, Catholic (lapsed), who made love energetically among the heather and the tall grass that filled the hollows between the ancient tumuli and giggled when a grasshopper landed on her naked skin.

The woman stirred in her bed and turned over. In the half-light Fergus could see how with a reflex motion her hand brushed back a strand of hair that had fallen across her mouth. 'Judith,' he said softly, 'Judith.' She did not respond but turned her face further into the pillow. The thin gold chain with the Star of David she insisted on wearing lay loosely on her skin. Her hand slipped and rested near the edge of the mattress. He leant over and touched it. It did not respond but neither did it withdraw into the shelter of the bedclothes. He moved his fingers gently over the back of her hand past the wristbone and on to the point where the fine dark hair began. She did not withdraw from the contact but neither did she respond to the pressure of his fingers. He left his hand there for a space that was measured by the rhythm of her breathing, which was, he felt, unnaturally controlled, regular but self-conscious. He counted to ten and then removed his hand, turning away. There was no longer any hope that she would raise the bedclothes and with a 'Come in' welcome him to the warmth of her belly and the strength of her thighs. With a sudden resolve he got up and began the ritual of the day, which would be another day of waiting. When he emerged from the shower in the corner of the room she was moving around in her nightdress, the plain loose shift through which, when she bent over, he could see the ripple of the vertebrae along the line of her strong muscular back. 'Hi,' he said. To which she answered with a 'Hi' that was purely ritual, uncommunicative, neutral, dismissive. He dressed quickly and followed the progress of her toilet – a process he knew by heart and one in which there would be no concealments, no false modesties, but a cool physical detachment as neutral as her morning greeting.

He is sitting on the side of his bed, looking at the map of this town, swept by winds off the sierra, where a Roman aqueduct leaps over the main road a hundred yards away from their hotel. He is familiar with the plan of the streets that rise up from the square for he has studied it carefully. He looks over to where she is gathering together her bits and pieces, scanning the room in her precise, orderly way – for orderliness is one of her great virtues – to be packed and ready in case they should decide to leave that morning. He has a chilling sense of the vacuum in which they live and move so close and so distant, but cannot any more than any other man venture into the interiority of her mind and being; for we are from our conception cut off from each other, so that even our moments of closeness are perhaps only an illusion and never more so than when our bodies interpenetrate.

'Why are you watching me?' she says, with an intonation of rebuke. She is angry and suspicious because the reasons that have brought her here are obscure to her, because she suspects that they have less to do with a recce for a documentary on the Peninsular War than with some aim he is withholding from her. For he has withheld much else in the time they have been together – five years now: so much that she has on occasion found herself screaming and beating at him with her fists in what he called a tantrum, as if her rage were a matter of hormonal levels and not a desperate attempt to break down the ramparts of his reserve, to find the springs of his thoughts and feelings, to discover what moved him apart from sex and (it seemed to her) a sort of kindness. A kindness she had accepted readily enough after the death of her husband (that absentee landlord of her heart). So it is with contained anger that she collects her discarded tights, her nightdress, her toilet things, and deftly packs them away. Not speaking. Determined, I imagine, not to speak. Controlling her rage.

Judith is a researcher; a handmaiden whose task it is to fetch and carry intellectual fodder for directors (male for the most part) no more talented than herself but endowed with a network of acquaintance that runs back through the services, through school, college and university. For them she is a skilled tracker-down of archival film, of a still photograph, of a print in an Edwardian fashion journal, mistress of an address book in which she can find with speed and accuracy – for they are clearly entered there in her firm, italianate hand – a speaker, a contact, a cultural guru, a military historian, an MP with the precise shade of Leftishness or Toryism appropriate to the programme she has been hired to service. Her reward: a credit in the end-titles where it will be read only by other professionals who may turn to a wife, a partner, a lover, an editor and say: 'Judith Gordon – wasn't she married to that ace cameraman, Kev what's his name, who flew too close to the north face of the Eiger? Remember that footage from the wreckage? You can see these two guys stuck there on the ledge. Freezing to death. Trying to wave. Then suddenly there's this amazing sort of pan and then nothing. Extraordinary stuff. Worked with her on that film I did about Machu Pichu. Great researcher – knows her job. Not my type though. A bit cold, a bit shut off I always thought. Well, good luck to her anyway.'

What she had been able to muster for her CV when she applied for his first job as a researcher was thin:
   1945-1951 South Hampstead High School for Girls
      (where her mother had been educated and of which
      she had few good memories)

1952-1955 London University – BA (2.1) Spanish
1955-1958 translator and interpreter FAO (Rome)
1958 – Office management – commercial translation –
assistant manager of a foreign language bookshop
Entries that ought to have had as a sub-text – more important than the manifest one – how at university, having cast off her mother's tutelage, she drank beer, lost her virginity, harvested melons on a kibbutz and was unhappy. Nothing about Itzak, the cause of that unhappiness, nor of her long attachment in Rome to a colleague, Sebastian, son of a Spanish Republican exile, of his infidelities, of the mess and pain of their parting, followed by a period of emptiness, of temping, of part-time jobs and loneliness. A time of occasional sexual encounters in her one-room flat on the ridge above Lavender Hill from which, on a clear day, you could look out and see beyond the steeples and domes of Kensington the heights of Hampstead where she went (as little as possible) to visit her mother, who lived with her lodgers and her cats in a dilapidated house with a garden that gave on to the Heath. It was the house from which she had been married and in which, when her husband disappeared, she had chosen to live out her self-imposed widowhood. Retired now from her job teaching English in a comprehensive school – 'not exactly la crème de la crème, I can tell you' – she found her pension and the rent from her lodgers – 'all professional people' – enough to keep her in gin-steeped gentility.

Then there had been Kev, the boy from West Kilburn, who had left school at fifteen and had no pretensions but a great knack of charming her mother and wakening in her some sort of maternal effection. His own mum had died when he was four and she claimed to see in him a certain orphaned look for which she forgave him his taste for tomato ketchup and bacon butties. Mercurial, constantly vanishing, returning to charm and seduce Judith with gifts of shells, a piece of Eskimo soapstone sculpture, a rhino-hair bracelet, a squat Indian figure which, he said, was a talisman against the plague and death. Inconstant, so seldom there that she had not bothered to move from her flat to which he brought his gear. Along with a tripod and cans of film it had lain piled in a corner of her bedroom where he checked and cleaned it obsessively. Watching him tend it she marvelled how, when he took it up, it seemed to become a part of him and understood why his mates called him 'the man with shock absorbers in his knees'. Even when the shot was hand-held, they said, you could bet it would be as steady as a rock. She learned how through the lens he could watch things happen, keep them in focus, frame them well – even if what he saw (it was on the Thai border) was a boy belching with fear as a bandit chief inter-rogated him and then signed to the guards who led him off to be clubbed to death. But when he stopped shooting he spewed his guts up, to the amusement of the ruler of those green and fertile hillsides from which the white powder found its way on to the streets of New York and London. Not unfaithful, except in the sense that he was unable to resist an assignation with danger; which was perhaps what had given a particular edge to their passion, a kind of fear that would flood through her like an orgasm as she lay beside him on long mornings and explored his body. It was a fear she had attempted to exorcise by marriage in a registry office where his mates clustered uneasily in the background. At the reception in a pub in Wardour Street her mother got tight and tearful, so that Kev had to comfort her and put her on a taxi to take her home to Hampstead. But the exorcism had not worked and when he did not return from an assignment in the Alps Judith was left with a sense of void, of lack, and of desire.

It was in that same one-roomed flat that she had first slept with Fergus, this man, this film-maker, whom she did not love as people seemed to understand 'love' but who had comforted her in her most desolate moments, who had taught her much professionally, with whom she worked and who was prepared – or so she felt in her better moments – to commit to her some part of his own essentially solitary life or such of it was escaped the demands of politics. For he belonged to a tightly organized and – as it seemed to her – paranoid party of the Left which (even after he had moved in with her) would summon him in the name of revolutionary discipline (and he would obey) to meetings at the Boatyard, its fortress-like headquarters (in which she had never been allowed to set foot), on the bank of an oily canal and which she suspected had sent him on this mission to Spain. So she was going to have to play her part in the charade of looking for locations, for paintings and engravings of the Peninsular War, of taking stills, just as – barely arrived in Madrid – she had found herself interpreting while Fergus attempted to interest in a co-production the Spanish television functionaries – sharply dressed, inscrutable behind their shades, and no doubt with more important matters on their minds now that the head of state lay near to death.

'Well, Fergus,' she asked as they sat after breakfast in the almost empty restaurant and watched the raindrops meander down the window-panes, 'are you going to tell me what we're doing here – or not?'

With his finger Fergus chased the crumbs of croissant over his plate.

'I have to wait for a contact. Either today or tomorrow.'

'One of your lot?'

'Yes, a comrade.'

'I don't suppose he's an expert on the Peninsular War – or is he?'

'I doubt it. Let's say it's party business.'

'Playing the usual games – long live the Fourth International and the World Revolution. Make-believe and paranoia.'

'No, it's for real. You've seen the papers. This country is on the knife-edge. But what I'm talking about is nothing out of the way. Very simple. Not really dangerous.'

She gave a little cough which was a tic she had when she was annoyed, upset, contrary.

'So I'm just a cover?'

'No,' he said, 'I need you.'

'Thank you very much, kind sir,' she responded ironically.

He looked at her with a sideways glance.

'You know what I mean – you're not just a cover – we got all this material. It'll come in handy when we get back.'

He patted the camera-case slung on a chair beside him. In it there were already stored pictures of walls where in smoke and flame the dead and wounded had hung with their feet caught in the rungs of the scaling ladders, of a huddled village where, after a battle, they had collected the plumes of the dead Highlanders in armfuls, of a long slope above a main road – a battlefield on which his shoe had kicked up a twisted cap-badge, French or British.

'That still makes me a cover.'

'If you want to put it like that. But I thought we were partners. I'd like you to be there – just in case. But they'll probably speak English. Like Carlos. You remember Carlos?'

She remembers a young man, student at some North London Poly, bearded, laconic, who had treated her with studied indifference and considerable suspicion; it had not prevented him from expecting her to translate long and involved accounts of sectarian debates within the Fourth

International. She recalls in particular his judgment on her father: 'A Stalinist.' To which she had no reply, for though she understood it, she did not speak the language of the great schism of the Left. Nor could she defend a man she had never known except from a bundle of photographs hidden away by her mother at the back of the tall dark desk in the living-room.

One day when she was twelve, her mother being safely out of the house, Judith had discovered and pressed a hinged panel in the desk and from its hiding-place removed a big envelope marked with the one word: Tony. What she found inside were photographs she had come to know by heart. Taking care not to disturb their sequence, she would lay them out on the table and try to read the images: images of a young man in flannels and an open-necked shirt, with the dark hair he had bequeathed her along with his strong features. Beside him there was usually a young woman (blonde, ash-blonde) with a roundish plump face but a slim waist. A cliff-top wind forced her cotton dress against her thighs as she raised a hand to control the fine hair that had blown across her face. It was the same young woman someone had snapped sitting on a rock in a Cornish cove, turning to smile at the camera. In her smile was openness and trust and a kind of sensuality. This was her mother, but Judith found it difficult to connect her with the discontented, physically aloof woman she knew. What she found even more improbable was to see her marching along what looked like the Embankment supporting a banner (red presumably) that said ARMS FOR SPAIN. The date on the back was 1936, the year when that unknown man, her father, had gone off to fight in Spain on the order of the Party, leaving a pregnant wife.

There were a couple of pictures from Spain of the same man with his mates – comrades, he would no doubt have called them, but she found the word difficult and could not imagine it on her mother's lips. In one they were mugging to the camera – a comrade with a tattoo on his arm had a bayonet in his teeth. Albacete, it said on the back – a name meaningless to her until much later, when she discovered that this was the base where the International Brigade had mustered before leaving for the front. In another he stood there alone, ghostly, almost disembodied in the fading black and white. Not solemn, smiling a little, he raised a clenched fist in salute, as if the rifle in his other hand was as harmless as the poles of the banners on that march along the Embankment to Trafalgar Square. Beyond that all she knew of him was that he had fought in the defence of Madrid and that he had been reported missing, presumed dead, in a battle in the valley of the Jarama.

Which meant he had deserted her before she was even born, so that at school she had always been the odd one out – the girl with no father – who had not only to confront the sense of being different but to suffer her mother's mute and rancid mourning. Into the bargain she had had to bear the migraines that had begun with her periods and when they came left her sick, white drawn, unable to do more than lie in a darkened room. At first her mother had insisted that they were something women simply had to put up with. 'There are worse things in life, I can tell you, my girl. Now you get up and take a good long walk on the heath, that'll soon blow your head-ache away.' But with time she had come to accept her daughter's stricken state, which Judith determined to regard as less an affliction – congenital perhaps – than as yet another thing to set her apart. Then there was her name: Judith Gordon. To her friends in junior school she boasted that her name was special, that she had had a Scottish daddy who had died in the war – a claim her mother did not exactly deny nor confirm, merely saying that Gordon was quite a common name, just look how many there were in the phone-book.

When she moved to her secondary school in Hampstead

she found herself to her joy in the same class as a girl called Susan Gordon. Was she Scottish, too? Judith asked of Susan, whose parents lived in Golders Green and had a delicatessen near Finchley Road tube station. Susan laughed and told her not to be silly. Judith was puzzled – even more so when she discovered that Susan was one of the group of half-a-dozen Jewish girls exempt from school prayers and religious instruction. Then there were the other girls who refused to take her claims to be 'Scottish' seriously, suggesting with giggles that she should prove it by dancing a Highland fling. She was, she felt, the victim of a double rejection. So she became unhappy, unwilling to go to school, indifferent to her mother's reproaches, to reminders of how lucky she was to have got a place in a good school and what a chance in life she was getting – not without sacrifices by her mother, who didn't exactly like teaching in a secondary modern. Was she unhappy at school? Were the other girls not nice to her? Didn't she get on with her form mistress? Were the lessons too difficult? Too much home-work? She would have to have a word with the headmis-tress.

Judith withdrew into a silence out of which she burst one morning with tears and snot and accusations: 'Some girls are making fun of me – saying I'm not Scottish at all. That I'm making it all up. That my real name is Cohen or Abrams. It isn't, is it?' 'No,' said her mother. Then with an unaccustomed gesture she put her arm round the girl, held and comforted her, drying her tears. 'Your name really is Gordon. Your father was called Tony Gordon. He was a Jewish boy from the East End.' That morning she did have a word over the phone with the headmistress: Judith wasn't very well – nothing serious – but she might have to be off school for a day or two.

When she recovered, Judith moved about the house as if trapped in a transparent bubble of silence, indifferent to her mother's pain and tears. Unforgiving. Over the next weeks she spent her hoarded pocket money on a Star of David. Her mother wept and begged her not to be silly but Judith wore it defiantly and at school claimed exemption from religious education and school prayers. Her headmistress consulted her mother and in view of the exceptional circumstances agreed to humour the girl; so she spent hours in a room with Susan Gordon and the other Jewish girls who, to her surprise, treated her with reserve and what felt like suspicion, asking her questions to which she did not know the answers, whispering and giggling among themselves. Stubbornly she continued to wear her Magen David as a challenge to a ghost. It was the same ghost that years later drove her – with her childhood and adolescence behind her – to go not like Fergus to a Wise Woman but to a man: South African (to judge by his clipped accent), Jewish, bearded, patient, understanding, questioning, before whom she (a grown woman who had suffered other wounds in life) had spilled out her child's rage at the man who had deserted her for a cause that embraced (it seemed) all humanity but had no room for his daughter.

Now, looking out at the rainy street, she asked: 'Suppose I don't feel like it?'

'Don't feel like what?'

'Like playing games.'

He ran his finger round the inside of the little carton of jam before sucking it carefully. It was a trick of behaviour she found distressing – the reflex of a greedy child, still unsatisfied in his fiftieth year of life, still oral, still hungry, for sex, for life and maybe death, which alone would sate his desperate desire for something final, filling, satisfying. It was what had once – but when last? – given an edge to their love-making, when she would play her part in his hungry exploration of her body that made her feel as if her sex were some succulent marine fruit. When she remembered these times she would find herself wondering (unbelievingly) whether her mother had played the same games with Tony, the Jewish boy, on the summer beaches, on cliff-tops, or in the cottage above the Cornish harbour where she herself had been conceived before her father took the road that led through France, then on across the Pyrenees by some high snow-filled pass and so at last to Albacete and the barracks of the International Brigade.

But certainly these were things she had once done with this familiar stranger who withdrew his finger from his mouth to say: 'I thought we had an agreement.'

That if she came to Madrid with him and then on to this provincial town he would go with her, if there was time, to Albacete *and* to the Jarama. The only thing he drew the line at was the monument to the dead of the Civil War high up on the Sierra. Even if it was supposed to contain the dead of both sides. Provided they were Catholics, naturally! He didn't need to go there to know what it would be like. With a great cross towering over the mausoleum built with the lives and slave labour of Republican prisoners, twenty thousand of them – what the regime called 'redemption through work'. Twenty years it took to complete. They quarried it, mined it by hand. The fine sharp dust of the granite lacerated their lungs. No doubt the old man who lay dying in Madrid would be buried there with all the pomp of the Church, the oratory and the Fascist flags, the Fascist salutes and the cries of 'Present!' when his name was called out. No thank you, he had no intention.

She got up and took her coat from the chair.

He wanted with a touch of anxiety to know when she would be back but all the satisfaction she would give him was: 'Some time.' Yet she took the trouble to ask at the desk if there were any messages. There were none. Yes, they would be sure to take a note if anyone called. *Como es que habla tam bien español, señorita?* asked the porter. Her reply was short and uncommunicative. She drew her raincoat round her and walked out into the square, then made her way up the steep streets towards where the aqueduct took off for its leap over the town. From the distance a squall of rain came on across the landscape until it stung her face. She turned away to explore the flagged streets, gently sloped to accommodate the traffic of horses, mules and donkeys. Even in the shops there were few people. This was a town that was unnaturally quiet, as if waiting for some event of moment or of danger.

Somewhere, in one of these very streets, a marvellous poet had lived modestly, sadly, thirty years before. Sebastian had introduced her to his work, for which she was grateful – it was one of the positive memories of their time together. She walked along with the vague, irrational hope that somehow she might recognize the house; she dared not ask one of the rare passers-by – the poet had been a Republican and had died in exile. In a wide square she stopped in front of a building, a kind of loggia, an open space separated from the pavement by an iron grille through which she could see on the flagstones wreaths of dead flowers, dusty immortelles with fading ribbons, red and black, lying beneath a bronze roll of honour to the fallen: *Caidos por Dios y por España.* A man stopped beside her – fiftyish, medium height, with a moustache that reminded her of the portrait of the Leader she had seen that morning above the porter's desk in the hotel. She wanted to turn away but his approach lacked sexual undertones and fear of discourtesy restrained her: *Usted es americana, verdad, señorita? Ah, inglés!* A monument to the Blue Division, he went on, '*volontarios – mi intende?* I too was in Russia – to fight against Bolshevism. Churchill now – a great man. But wrong to fight Hitler and not Bolshevism.' She began to disentangle herself, remarking that she didn't know much about politics. Then the thought came to her that this man with his courtesy, his genuine desire to inform a foreigner, his frankness, was of her father's age and generation. He would have undoubtedly fought against the Republic – a red-beretted soldier from Navarre perhaps – one of the warriors of Christ the King. As such he might have aimed the gun, fired the shot, given the order that killed her father. She was seized by sudden fear and revulsion and cutting short his compliments on her Spanish almost ran towards where the cathedral and its tower rose high above the rock on which the ancient town sat, limpet-like. At the very tip of the rock, at the Alcazar, turreted, curiously Disney-like, she turned back along the walls, watchful and cautious, and so back (reluctantly) towards the hotel where her partner was waiting.

Our relationships are not logically patterned – rather, they are a ravelled skein of hopes, fears, fantasies and needs, of impulses of generosity, of ravening hunger for affection, of deceptions of oneself and the other, of false consciousness, of incomprehensions, of misreadings of a word, a gesture, a sexual advance, of promises made and forgotten, of reticences and avowals, of moments of joy, sharing, giving and taking, of wounds suffered and inflicted. If by accident or intent we pick at one of the tangled threads and pull until it runs free, the whole fabric may disintegrate.

As she walked slowly down from the old town, Judith was aware that her work of unravelling her relationship with Fergus was far advanced; that what held her back from the last unpicking, from the word that would be decisive, was as much as anything the thought of her mother sitting with her chihuahua in her lap and a g-and-t in one hand saying she had never understood what Judith saw in Fergus – who was hardly ever there anyway – worse if anything than that Spanish boy in Rome – Sebastian – and God knows he had been a disaster – not that one man was any better than another – although poor Kevin was different – she still couldn't get over that terrible accident – but what good had marriage done her – and sex (if that was what Judith got out of her relationships in inverted commas) was one of the most overvalued activities ever invented. So maybe Judith would settle down at last, get herself a pension, get a decent flat, make herself comfortable, enjoy herself, travel, go to the theatre, and surely she could find some women friends to share things with – not that she agreed with all this talk about liberation but, be honest, did Judith really need a man?

In the hotel bedroom Fergus sat and read the latest number of the party's theoretical journal. The text was dense, heavily footnoted, the issues theological in their subtlety. He felt uneasily that there was a remoteness in these pages from the stuff of living politics – from the situation here in Spain, where the whole country waited for a death in fear and hope. The maid had come and gone, soft-footed, deft, making the beds, tidying, excusing herself – a country girl, he guessed, with a red birthmark on her neck only half-hidden by her hair. She completed her work expeditiously and left with a slight smile. He laid down his reading and raised the slat of the blind to look towards the town and the aqueduct. He was doubly anxious. What if Carlos or some-one in his place made contact with him – would Judith be back in time to interpret? But more importantly, what would he do if he were expected to go beyond handing over the document – the Venezuelan passport – which was hidden in the lining of his camera-case?

It was a question he had been asking himself ever since he flew out from Heathrow. He had come through cus-toms and immigration into the dictator's Spain with a mix-ture of excitement and anxiety, the sensation he had first experienced during the abortive journey across the plains of north-east Europe towards a battle that had died away before he could be caught up in it and test his fear. In his profession as film-maker he had since sought that sensation on assignments in troubled, bloodstained and murderously dangerous locations. But he knew that they lacked the cutting edge of battle.

At the far end of the corridor a door banged and someone shouted incomprehensibly. Fergus listened for a little then, rising, he drew from the side pocket of his holdall a notebook labelled PENWAR. He flipped over the pages till he found the passage he wanted, words to be spoken over shots of a misty hilltop: the words of a rifleman, literate, intelligent, member of an élite corps, recalling how he had waited at dawn for the French columns to storm uphill towards the British line at a place in Portugal called Bussaco.

On such occasions little or no conversation passes. The privates generally lean upon their firelocks and the officers on their swords; and few words are wasted. The faces of the bravest change colour and their limbs tremble not with fear but anxiety while watches are consulted till the individuals who consult them absolutely weary of their employment. On the whole it is a situation of high excitement and darker, deeper feeling than any other in human life.

It was his desire – it had become almost a craving – for the adrenalin fix of fear that had moved him that evening little more than a week before when, in an elegantly bare room with front windows that gave on to the solid sweep of a Victorian crescent, the man standing by the door with his hands in the pockets of his leather jacket called the group to order with the one word, 'Comrades'. His gravelly voice had in its time sold everything on television from breakfast cereals to fast cars ('but *never* holidays in Spain'). 'Comrades, we have been asked to hold this meeting to discuss an urgent and important matter of Party business with a leading comrade, Comrade Fred, who as you all know is a member of the Central Committee of the Party. Comrade Fred.'

Comrade Fred – the conventions of the Party demanded that second names be suppressed in the interests of security – was sitting in a big chair with his back to the windows. Soberly dressed. Suit, tie, carefully polished shoes. He might have been a low-grade civil servant – not well off, limited in his taste, curiously petty bourgeois in his appearance, Fergus thought with a sense of guilt at passing judgement in such terms on a comrade of thirty years standing, a man who had sacrificed everything for the Party, accepting its disciplines and its regime.

'Well, comrades,' Comrade Fred began in his slightly nasal Edinburgh accent, 'I have asked for this meeting for a very special purpose. I am going to test your political maturity. To see whether your commitment goes any further than the easy jobs: collecting for the fighting fund, selling the paper, speaking up – and I know you do speak up – at union meetings. But the girls in my office at the Boatyard do as much and more. And what do you risk? Not much. No one is going to put you out on the stones because you are members of the Fourth International. All right you might be blacked here or there. But you intellectuals can always find ways round it, can always buck the system, can't you? Come on – I've been around. I know how the system works. You've all got friends – class friends in the TV companies and at the Beeb. They won't see you go hungry. You are not going to starve. Not going to be thrown back on Social Security. Now the Party doesn't blame you for that, and neither do I, as someone who has spent a lifetime in the struggle. We recognize that objectively speaking this is your social and economic situation and there is not much to be done about it till we come to power as the vanguard of the proletariat of this country and

25

the world. And believe me, comrades, the show is on the road. It's coming. Not today or tomorrow. But the old dialectical process is working away out there, throwing up contradictions in the capitalist system. Opening up spaces for our Party to lead the working class to socialism. You do believe that don't you, eh, comrades? Let me tell you the truth. I sometimes wonder just how strong your commitment is to the cause, how much you would be willing to risk for the movement – which is an international one, let me remind you, with comrades in every country in Europe and beyond. Now you have all met some of these comrades who have come here to the Party school and will know that they are men and women who have been thoroughly tested in the struggle because in their countries there are no soft opinions – not the kind you have – and when they take on Party work they risk their lives. Like real revolutionaries. They're not playing games, comrades.'

Siobhan, the young woman in whose house they were meeting, raised her hand. She was in her early thirties but still looked girlish with her round freckled face, pale blue eyes and fine red hair. It straggled down to curl on her white neck; elsewhere on her body – as Fergus had learned – it was a down that glinted on the pallor of her skin. To the coach-trade public she was the star of a series of farces in which she shed her clothes with a kind of disdain, but for the comrades she was chiefly notable as a speaker who with passion and conviction, with urgency and warmth, sometimes teasing, sometimes hectoring, would urge an audience to 'dig deep' for the paper, for the fighting fund, exhorting them as the stewards passed the orange plastic buckets round in cinemas, theatres, in some park, to remember the comrades in Lebanon, in Chile, the strikers of Grunwick, Merseyside or Glasgow. An act, Judith had said the one time she had agreed to attend a rally at the Hammersmith Odeon, a display of histrionics. But Fergus had dismissed the comment as a reflex of jealousy for he had once confessed that he found Siobhan with her freckles sexually attractive; and had added – jokingly, dismissively, dishonestly – that naturally there could be no question of having an affair with a comrade. To which Judith had replied that sometimes he seemed to think she was appallingly innocent. And there they had left it.

Now Comrade Siobhan was asking with a voice that retained a Celtic softness whether Comrade Fred could be more precise. She was sure that every member of the branch would be prepared to take on any task the Party entrusted to them.

Comrade Fred listened indulgently – he always listened indulgently to Siobhan, which led some of the comrades to hint that there was or had been some sexual trade-off between them – and as he listened looked round the circle that sat before him in the spacious first floor room, with its bare polished floor, the prints of Che Guevara on the walls and the Tiffany lamp on the fine gate-legged table. To the back a French window gave on to the enclosed communal space, the private park, where an au pair watched as Siobhan's children played hide-and-seek in the shrubbery. Their voices and laughter rang clear as glass, middle-class and confident, into the quiet of the Sunday morning. When they died away the group could hear the plash of water in a fishpond under the garden wall.

Comrade Fred looked round the group – ten of them in all, of whom Fergus was probably the oldest. Because he had chosen to sit with his back to the light, Comrade Fred's face was shadowed. It was a strong face, prognathous, smooth-shaven, ruddy – unhealthily so because of long hours spent in committee rooms, at branch meetings, in offices, in the printing shop where the Party paper slid down from the press to be bundled for distribution, sold by Fergus and his comrades but in any case (sold or unsold) paid for to the last copy. Above the ruddy face the hair was thick, grey and stubbled. The hairline began high on the forehead, leaving bare a curious indentation in the bone which was said by the members of the Party's inner circle to be the result of a blow from a truncheon in pre-war Hamburg where, as a merchant seaman, the comrade had fought the Nazis in the narrow streets of the docklands by the Elbe. Fergus knew that when the comrade stood up he would be surprisingly small with short, slightly bowed legs and a rolling gait. His hands, resting on the arms of the chair, were small too and curiously podgy.

'Yes, comrade, I am sure the will is there. But the will is merely something in the mind, in the consciousness. It can be merely a question of dreams and aspirations. Fantasies. What the Party needs is the will plus the determination to convert it into action. In concrete terms. In the real world.'

Somewhere on another floor the telephone rang and rang unanswered. Comrade Fred cocked his head and listened till the ringing stopped. Fergus heard someone light up and became aware of the unmistakeable smell of grass. But Comrade Fred, usually quick to condemn such manifestations of decadence as long hair and the smoking of dope appeared not to notice – perhaps chose not to. He was drumming with his podgy fingers on the arms of his chair. Then he spoke again.

'The comrades will be aware – even the bourgeois press has had to report it but there is a full account from our Spanish comrades in tomorrow's edition of the paper – that in its death-throes Spanish Fascism has embarked on a wave of harsh repression. Last month they executed comrades with whom we had our differences, but there are moments when we have to show solidarity on the Left, in the same way as the Spanish workers have shown theirs. You will see from the paper that last week 100,000 workers came out on strike. Why? Because thirty comrades had been condemned to death.

'Now let me tell you something about the methods of the rotten dictatorship this man Franco has presided over with the approval of big business, the Church, the armed forces, the British government, the Americans with their air-bases and their aircraft carriers at anchor in Malaga – all there to keep the Iberian peninsula safe for Rio Tinto Zinc and Fiat and the other multinationals who have their hands on the Spanish economy. Well, there was a pregnant woman among the condemned comrades. She was spared because of her unborn child – the Roman Church, as we know, is always very concerned about the unborn child. Once it's born that's another matter. It can starve to death. Be killed by poverty and neglect. But not in the womb. No comrades, not in the womb. So the mother's death sentence has been commuted to thirty years in prison. And thirty years means thirty years. They don't joke, these gentlemen. That means she'll not on their reckoning be out until into the new century. And the child will be brought up in some Catholic orphanage in the grip of priests or nuns, in superstition and reaction. But the great thing, comrades, is this: they can never be sure. Maybe that child will emerge to fight for its class and for the revolution. Stranger things can happen. After all, you people are here today. Members of a party of the working class.'

Comrade Fred looked round and chuckled while his audience fidgeted. 'But, comrades, the Christian gentlemen who run the country aren't just considerate about babies – they're considerate with adults, too. Shall I tell you how? Can you guess?'

Down below a door slammed and children's feet came running up the stairs to the landing outside the room. Comrade Fred paused for a moment as the au pair's voice forbade them entry and urged them on up the stairs. Fergus followed their steps as they ran past Comrade Siobhan's bedroom. When he first came close to the Party – four, no five years ago – he had known it as somewhere warm and safe, cut off from the black ghettos, from the favelas and shanty towns, from a world of poverty and death.

'No? Then let me spell it out to you. The condemned men were given the choice between the garotte and the firing squad. You don't know what the garotte is? Let me tell you that too. You are put on a kind of chair with a stake at the back. There's a steel collar attached to the stake. They put it round your neck. The executioner twirls a hand-screw, the collar tightens, strangles you and breaks your neck. The comrade whose wife got thirty years chose the firing squad. Do you blame him? Now we have learned – we have our contacts – that our Spanish comrades need help to get a member of their central committee out of the country. All he needs are good papers. We have the papers. Don't ask how. We need to get them into the right hands. Urgently. Now, comrades, you are people who travel a lot, professionally, of course,' (Comrade Fred grinned ironically) 'so I want you to get a volunteer to do the courier job for the Party.'

Comrade Fred rose and picked up the briefcase from beside his chair. The young woman who was his driver and who had sat silently observing the group as he spoke rose at the same time. Her way of looking down and away from people's faces marked her, thought Fergus, as an ex-convent girl who had acquired from the nuns the habit of chastity of the eyes.

'Now I'll leave you to sort it out among yourselves. I want the name of a volunteer by this evening at the latest. *Salud, compañeros.*' With a clenched fist salute that was only half-mocking he walked out of the room. The young woman followed chastely in silence. From where he sat Fergus could see them come out on to the pavement and climb into a dark saloon car, the young woman at the wheel, Comrade Fred in the back.

'Right, comrades, you've all heard what Comrade Fred had to say to us,' the comrade with the gravelly voice began. 'We are being tested as we've never been tested before. Forget about selling the paper. Forget about last

Sunday's demo when incidentally some comrades were missing without explanation and had better have a good excuse, because Comrade Fred is not happy. Not happy at all. But this time our revolutionary commitment is on the line. Now as a party we are – as you all know – against adventures, against individual exploits. We leave that sort of thing to the anarchists and petty bourgeois romantics. But this is a special case. I am going to give you five minutes to think it over. Then I shall ask someone to come forward. I know some of you have commitments – professional commitments, family commitments. But your first commitment is to the Party and to the International of which you are all members.'

In the silence that followed, people fidgeted. Comrade Siobhan rose to leave the room and her voice could be heard calling up the stairs – soft, modulated, maternal, Irish – saying Mummy wouldn't be long, that she had a special treat for them if they would just be good children.

When she returned, the man in the leather jacket had taken over Comrade Fred's chair.

'Well,' he said, 'which comrade is it to be?'

Later Fergus could not easily explain either to himself or to Judith what had prompted him to raise his hand.

'Comrades,' he said, 'I am working on a project and need to do a recce in Spain. It may never come to anything – you know how it is. One of these historical jobs – a documentary on the Peninsular War.'

The man with the gravelly voice laughed.

'Well,' said Fergus defensively, 'that was when the Spaniards invented the idea of the guerilla war. I could leave by Wednesday.'

'Alone?' Comrade Siobhan asked sharply.

Fergus knew what she meant.

'Well, no I'd take a researcher with me to look at locations. And as an interpreter.'

'Comrade,' said Siobhan coldly, 'you know there are

problems – political ones – about your partner. We have discussed them before.'

'Right,' said the man in the leather jacket, disregarding her intervention, 'I move we accept Comrade Fergus's offer – subject to the approval of the Central Committee, naturally. I shall report to Comrade Fred this afternoon. Now, comrades, there's one other item on the agenda. Sales of the paper. The record of this branch is deplorable. You all know the reasons. Lack of enthusiasm. Excuses. Laziness. Political wavering. Sloppy thinking. The Central Committee has decided that as from next week the target for sales will be increased by twenty-five per cent. No, there will be no discussion. Comrade Fergus, you will report to Comrade Fred at the Boatyard this evening.'

Fergus got up from the bed and went to the window. The wind was still gusting. Rain rattled briefly on the glass. Somewhere in the houses that rose up to the hill where the aqueduct launched itself across the valley there might be a comrade waiting for a favourable moment to make contact with him. This was the right hotel, of that he was sure. But suppose the comrade did not come, suppose he had been picked up by the security forces? Since the man who lay dying in Madrid had been struck down by a heart attack at a cabinet meeting three weeks ago, there had been arrests – which was only to be expected. Twiddling the knobs on their portable radio to cut out the static, they had learned from the BBC's World Service that the Pope had condemned what His Holiness had described as 'harsh repression'. Things must be bad, Fergus had commented. But Judith said there was no mention of his message anywhere in the Spanish papers, which were dominated by solemn and anodyne bulletins, the same ones as were read by the radio and television announcers as if they were speaking from the antechamber of the room where the great man lay dying.

Fergus went over to turn on the radio and fiddled till he got the BBC again, but there was merely a discussion on the Labour Party, the TUC and the wage freeze. Stale exchanges, he thought with his fingers on the knob, debates from the talking-shop of parliament that didn't begin to look at the record of the reformist trade union leaders or to discuss their refusal to give a lead to the working class they were supposed to represent. He switched off. What could you expect? he asked himself; at its last conference the Labour Party had voted against a motion to nationalize the major industries, the banks, the insurance companies and land. But it had passed by a show of hands a voluntary restraint on wages.

Turning away he saw that Judith had left beside the rest of their luggage the huge leather satchel she had acquired on some trip to Jutland – a postman's bag, travel-stained, polished from use, her vast hold-all, her private resource in which he now (idly and guiltily) rummaged and produced her address book. Bulky, worn with use, packed with names and annotations, cancellations and cross-references, it bulged against the press-stud fastener. In the bottom of the bag there were only the usual crumpled tissues, a half-empty book of matches, a couple of tampons, a torn packet of aspirin, a letter from some friend from her Roman days, old bus and tube tickets, a comb, nail polish: the detritus of her daily life. In an inner pocket in the side of the bag the air-line tickets. Madrid to LHR. Not valid after 20 November. That left almost a week. So, masses of time. Her passport. On the pale blue pages with their white watermarking border police had set their stamps, purple, red, pink, sometimes with geometrical precision, sometimes at haphazard angles: Kon. Marechaussee Nederland, A magyar népköztársaságra, US Immigration Authorities and – most recently – Direccion Seg. Estado. From the photograph she looked out at him with a startled expression. The rest of the strip of photographs from which the image came were stuck in a corner of the notice-board in her basement kitchen in Highbury, labelled 'Wanted by Interpol'.

The flat lighting conveyed little of the strength of her features, the rather prominent cheekbones, the way her thick black hair, parted in the middle, framed the pallor of her face with its curls: a Mediterranean (Jewish?) face, except for the blue eyes she had from her mother. The details on the opposite page he knew by heart: name of bearer – Miss Judith Gordon; national status – British subject: profession/occupation – researcher; place of birth – London; date of birth – 20/2/37; height – 5 ft 6; distinguishing marks – none; children – none, because she didn't want any. Which was why, somewhere in her belongings, there would be a strip of silver-foil on which only one or two pink pills were likely to be left.

The subject had come up only a couple of weeks before, in a moment of tension when he was more than usually aware that she was floating away from him like an ice-floe in spring and in a panic he had asked why they didn't have a kid. She had wanted to know why on earth she should throw up her job just when she was getting somewhere professionally, had been promised a chance to direct something, nothing great – a couple of magazine items for a women's programme – but a beginning. In any case she didn't think children should be brought into the world just to patch up ropey relationships. Then with the logicality that had once delighted but now increasingly irritated him, she had pointed out that as far as she could see he hadn't shown much interest in starting a family with any of his other ladies and didn't see why she should pander to his patriarchal longings.

As he returned the passport to its pocket, Fergus's fingers felt something: a thin notebook, ring-backed, nothing on the yellow cover although Judith had a habit – a mania he had called it sometimes – of labelling everything. It was, she pointed out, the sort of thing women had to learn to do. Because men were too bloody lazy and expected women to do the chores for them. Inside in her neat, orderly hand there were notes, short paragraphs interspersed with scribbled colophons – what looked like notes from her research but other jottings as well. As he began to read, he was aware of a mixture of fear and excitement. It reminded him of the time when he had gone through his mother's dressing-table and found there a rubber contraption and a tube of some sort of cream. He was fifteen. The thought that his mother allowed herself to be shagged, screwed or even (but it was not a word he would have dared to use himself) fucked had bewildered him. From now on he would know as he looked at her over the breakfast table that she allowed the red-faced man stuck away behind his paper to do things to and with her in bed.

War : What is it about men and war? Is it just excitement? Escape? Their need to prove themselves? Travel? Join the modern army and see the world!

★　★　★

Does F. fuck around? I expect so. Do I mind? I don't know. What does that say about us?

What did Mum do about sex? Did she really never have a boyfriend?

The bastard. Leaving her like that.

If F. left me. What would I do? Probably try abstinence for a while. Like after Sebastian took off.

★　★　★

What I suspect more and more are those people who love their fellow-human beings in the abstract but don't give a damn about the havoc they commit in the lives of those around them.

★　★　★

Men think a good fuck settles everything. Knock themselves out and fall asleep. Great.

What would F. do if I just said No? Howl like a great baby I expect.

Maybe it's sex they're after when they join up. Girlfriends in foreign parts, whores, brothels, rape. v. the British troops in the PenWar.

The siege and taking of Badajoz (Ciudad Rodrigo? check!). There was rape, looting and murder. They tore the earrings from women's ears and cut off the rings from their fingers.

'The scenes that took place in the town were frightful and not fit to be recorded. (!) The priests took refuge with the fair sex in the great churches for safety. There was no safety anywhere . . . But still the truth must be told – the besieging army was promised the sacking of the town when taken and notwithstanding all the devotion and bravery of the British soldier, this promise of pillage adds to his courage and determination.'

How can I speak for my sisters?

I must try.

Wellington gave them three days. Then he had the provost marshall put up a gallows in the main square and hang a few.

Note: Find a portrait (daguerreotype?) of Lady Smith, the fourteen-year-old girl who fled with her sister from the sack of Badajoz, was sheltered by a young officer, married him and as wife of the Governor General of the Cape gave her name to the town of Ladysmith.

F. says that the most important thing about Badajoz is the way Franco's Moorish troops machine-gunned the Republican prisoners in the bullring.

★ ★ ★

What do men expect from sex? Mum always says they are like randy dogs running through the streets looking for a bitch on heat.

(The trouble is she thinks I'm a bitch.)

Why should they be so desperate and full of needs?

F. gets his kicks from taking risks. I think.

So far he has been lucky. Why involve me?
More important – why did I let myself get involved?

* * *

Seb. was very macho. His father gave him money to go to a brothel when he was fifteen. Making a man of him.
Macho politics. Men who know all the answers. The avant-bloody-garde.

* * *

That man Fred with his car and his woman driver.
Comrade Siobhan. F. fancies her. Always has done. Getting dolly bird parts, Always having to strip off. Vulnerable as hell.
What about me? After Kevin crashed. So needy. Open.
What about Annabelle? What do I know about her except the odd remark.
He's supposed to be on the Left. So why these upper-class girlfriends?

* * *

That statue by Donatello in the Loggia dei Lanzi in Florence. Judith and Holofernes. The way she holds her sword. The way she has her foot planted on Holofernes. The wound on his neck. Not angry. Strong.
'The trauma she must feel is revealed by her open mouth and unfocussed stare. Donatello's figure is a testimony to J's piety and to her humanity.' (Check quote – source?)
Powerful. Beautiful. Covered in bird-shit but still amazing. Seb. hated it. Woman as the killer, castrator. The same name as me. It frightened him.

Fergus sat for a moment with the notebook open before him. Italy he barely knew. He had memories of a baking piazza in August during his honeymoon with Sarah. Their bedroom window looked out on to the Lungarno. As they made love in the hot afternoons they could hear the water spilling over the concrete dam where the young men lay and displayed themselves in the sun. A cheap hotel in those days. Had Judith and Sebastian stayed in the same one? He would ask her one day, just out of curiosity. Not jealousy. Sebastian was a remote, shadowy figure.

39 this year. The clock is beginning to wind down.

I dreamt I was in a house – not sure whose – full of rooms – I was looking for something – a doll I think – I went up the stairs and into the bedroom. There was a man there. A big beard. Wearing a Magen David. When I ran up to him it was only a scarecrow. Too bloody obvious. Maybe I made it up.

Identity. I need an identity. I need my Star. Itzak could have helped me. F. calls me a Zionist. I'm not. Not anything maybe.

(Who the hell was Itzak, Fergus asked himself.)

★   ★   ★

Spain. I'm afraid of Spain.
I wish I could trust F. But less and less.
Must talk soon.
Just like my father. The Party says go to Spain and he goes to Spain A different party. The same reflex of obedience.
What for?
Boys' games. A sort of basic irresponsibility. Childish.
A PenWar subaltern: 'It is by no means the least pleasing circumstance in the life of a soldier upon active service that he never knows when he wakes in the morning where he will sleep at night. Once set in motion and like any other machine he moves till the power that regulates his movement calls a halt; and wherever that halt may occur, there for the present is his home.'
The same man: 'I have always been struck by the great coolness of the women before an advance. I feel the sort of life they lead, after they have for any length of time, followed the army in the field, sadly unsexes them. 60 women only being permitted to accompany a battalion they are, of course, perfectly secure of obtaining as many husbands as they choose; hence few widows of

soldiers continue in a state of widowhood for any unreasonable time; so far, indeed, they are a highly favoured class of female society.' (!) So not just groupies like the girls at that meeting in the Hammersmith Odeon.

And, God forbid, not like the French army which 'is encumbered with a host of improper females.' (Sir John Fortescue)

The voice of male fear of women unchanged over the years.

The women. Were they complicit? Had they no other choice? Did they find some extraordinary freedom in licensed polyandry.

Supposing this documentary actually gets made who will speak for these women?

I suppose I can trust F. not to make a piece glorifying militarism – all uniforms and battle honours and shots of that horsed artillery unit that fires its guns in fancy dress in Hyde Park on the Queen's birthday.

Another officer: 'Spanish ladies in general are very fine figures, for which reason, as I have been told, their undergarments, far from flowing, are very narrow and tied down the front with many knots of finest silk ribbon.'

I like the hypocritical aside – 'as I have been told'.

★   ★   ★

Era una noche de verano
– estaba abierto el balcon
y la puerta de mi casa –

It was a summer night
The balcony was open;
so too my house door;
death came in.
It goes up to her bed
it passes me without looking;
then with delicate fingers
breaks something frail.
Silent, without a glance,
death passes once more

before me. What have you done?
Death did not reply.
My child was there at peace,
my heart full of pain.
Ay! what death broke
was a thread between the two of us.

Ay! lo que la muerte ha roto
era un hilo entre los dos.

★   ★   ★

I just happen to think that there are some experiences. The loss of love, the loss of a father, someone's death (K's), which are probably an enduring and unchanging part of human experience. F. says this is naïve. That there is no such thing as a universal human condition. It's a sentimental idea, he says. Our frame of mind, our emotions, our reactions to situations are conditioned by the society in which we have been brought up.

★   ★   ★

At least with Seb. I didn't need to translate everything.
How much Spanish did my father know? Salud, compañero.
No pasaran. *Did he shout* guapa *at the girls from the back of the truck as they drove to the war?*
Why should it still hurt damn it? I'm not a child any more. No one to speak to. Can't speak to F. No going back to that fucking man with the beard.
I think maybe I've missed my period. I wonder how he'd react.
Why do I stay with F? What's in it for him? For me?
I feel more and more shut out. Used. Used for sex. Used as a cover.
He'd always have 'the comrades'. Like my Dad.

★   ★   ★

Alarm over. I'm not pregnant. 'The redcoats' have arrived. That's what that bastard Flaubert, terrified of fatherhood, kept wanting to hear from poor old Louise Colet who wrote bad poetry and loved him. Whom he exploited emotionally and sexually. 'Redcoats' – very appropriate – very PenWar.

★ ★ ★

The sound of a footstep in the corridor alerted Fergus. He dropped the notebook into the bottom of the bag and rose from the bed as Judith entered.

'Any news?' said Judith as she took off her raincoat and hung it by the door.

Fergus shook his head. 'You were a long time,' he said.

She had been looking for something. A house. She knew it was there but felt she couldn't ask – why not? because the man who had lived was Antonio Machado – a great poet and a Republican. Who wrote some rather boring political poems. About Russia. And some great love poems.

'Why must political poetry be boring?'

'I never said that. I just don't think his political poems are very good. Listen – he spoke up for the Republic when it was dangerous to speak out and he died in exile. But the most important event in his life was this: when he was thirty-five he married a girl of fifteen. Two years later, she died of TB. You know what he said? He said that death came in one summer night – no listen! – and with delicate fingers broke the thread between them.'

'I think you told me once before.'

'Maybe I did. Then when he was fifty-three he fell in love with another women, a poet.'

'What do you think he did in between? Live like a monk? I bet he was a regular at the local brothel.'

She disregarded his interruption.

'This time it was the Civil War that broke the thread. But you're not listening.'

He was listening, it was simply that he didn't find such individual sadnesses of much interest when you put them against what was going on then – or now. Take the situation in Spain today. . . .

'Sometimes,' she interrupted him, 'I can't help thinking you and your lot are like the Moonies.'

This was her latest line, first spoken half in jest, now repeated seriously, in bitterness.

There are exchanges between lovers, partners, friends, that are complex formal rituals. They can be gambits but more often they are endgames. It is only gradually, however, that we may come to recognize them for what they are: sterile repetitions. Fergus and Judith I imagine as past (or grand) masters in such exchanges, that at best end in a draw or a stalemate. For both had acquired skill from practice: she with Sebastian, he with Sarah.

By the time he was demobbed, Fergus had entered on a long engagement – three years – while he slogged through a degree in history at Cambridge among returned soldiers older than himself, men who (given the smallest audience) recounted selections from their memories, stories exciting or harrowing, worked at, polished, and now told with cool bravado to illustrate the grotesque farce of war.

So there are these two Gurkhas pissing themselves laughing in the back of the truck and all sorts of shit flying about and when I ask what the hell there was to laugh at guess what they said. 'But, sahib, doesn't the corporal look funny with no head!' I ask you! But he's a bloody good soldier, Johnny Gurkha. Yes, I will have another.

Meanwhile Sarah had found a job with a publisher and an attic flat behind the British Museum where they recaptured some of the excitement of their lovemaking in the North

German heathlands. That they would get married once he had a job was taken for granted and married they were when he became junior history master in his (and his father's) old school under the Downs. The wedding in his Cambridge College Chapel was a compromise, a gesture to her Catholic upbringing. To it came her father – the withdrawn, precise widower (an Oxford man himself) who had received Fergus in his chambers and interrogated him thoroughly but politely over a glass of very dry sherry.

At the wedding reception he managed, with some distaste, to exchange a few words with Fergus's father, rubicund, half-sloshed, with the angry scar on his cheek where a bayonet had glanced off the bone in that other war; the freelance journalist who (alongside contributions to a variety of provincial papers) did pieces for the BBC's Overseas Services on whatever came his way: British institutions, the Monarchy, the Lord Mayor's Show, swan-upping, Changing the Guard, the pageantry of London Town, the Highland Show – what the listeners (he doubted that there were any) were led to believe constituted 'the British way of life'.

Of his wedding day Fergus remembered chiefly his father's reproaches – why wasn't he wearing a kilt? was he ashamed of being a MacIver or what? and his mother's sad, nervous attempts, hat slightly askew, to talk to Sarah's father and her profuse apologies over a glass of spilt wine; the way she wandered off to inspect the College's herbaceous borders. It was in the tending of her garden, the bedding, the transplanting, the division of roots, the clipping and pruning, that she found a sense of order and continuity to set against the disorder of her husband's ramshackle finances. Remembered too his father-in-law's speech which, it seemed to Fergus, concealed a threat under its jokiness about how Fergus was about to take from him his dear daughter to share what lawyers liked to call (in the decent obscurity of a dead language, he should add) *mensa et thalamus*, which, if he knew his Latin and his law, meant something more than bed and board. He could only hope – if he might coin a phrase – that all their troubles might be little ones. But there had been no little ones because of Sarah's presumed barrenness.

What there had been was (for Fergus) a spell of teaching at his old school, a mock-gothic building with cloisters that echoed noisily with black-coated boys and masters in academic gowns. Fergus's Rector had retired. His successor was in his forties – tall, gangly, sharp featured with a slight lisp which only the most daring boys would imitate and then only in moments of absolute safety; OBE, DSO, it said after his name on the noticeboard outside his study. He had been something in Intelligence, which many pupils and parents equated with spies and Buchanesque adventures; he had in fact made his military reputation by applying his pedantry, his obsession with detail, to the analysis of German High Command signals' traffic dealing with shipments of petrol and oil from Italy to Rommel's Afrika Korps. He saw his main function as that of maintaining the college's reputation by recruiting to it the sons of actors and writers and the grandsons of retired military men from the neighbouring South Coast resorts; there was also the task of stamping out the split infinitive and the expression 'under the circumstances' which, as anyone with the least smattering of Latin must know, could only be 'in the circumstances'. 'Circum,' he would say at assembly, 'around. So not *under – in*. Accuracy in the use of the English language is one way of protecting our national heritage. Remember that what you speak is the language of Shakespeare and do not degrade it with sloppy usage and horrible Americanisms. So *in* the circumstances.'

Although it was rumoured that he had never seen action of any kind, he was a passionate enthusiast for the cadet corps with a march past on parents' day when, at the side of some general with red collar patches, he scanned the ranks, spotted any slackness and remedied it with extra parades. One boy unwise enough to write an article for the school mag stating his conscientious objections to joining the corps was threatened with expulsion. Only the fact that his father was a BBC mandarin saved him. Fergus was incautious enough to suggest at a staff meeting that the boy might have a case. He was carpeted immediately after the meeting and told that the Rector could not possibly countenance such attitudes in the staff who were, after all, expected to maintain standards and set an example to the boys committed to their charge – not to encourage adolescent posturings. Perhaps Fergus might want to consider his position; which Fergus did and, after consulting the BBC mandarin with the pacifist son, applied for and got a job at the BBC and so made it into television at its moment of expansion.

All this time Sarah had been stuck away, as she put it, in a cottage under the Downs. She had found nothing to occupy her in the nearby village, had avoided co-option into the whole business of church fairs and other good works but had dutifully attended school functions and found the Rector's Welsh wife terribly uninteresting. Boredom weighed upon her as did her presumed barrenness. One or other or both together had made her take to gin and to an affair with a neighbouring farmer – ex-Long Range Desert Group – who swore that Britain had become impossible to live in. He was going to emigrate to Rhodesia where there was land and space and people who still had standards.

When Fergus began to commute to London the end-games began in earnest. With accusations on Sarah's part that he was sleeping around. With excuses on his part for lost trains, absences blamed on location work, on editing sessions, on conferences, and nights spent sleeping on the floor in various flats in London. No, nothing to do with sex. Work, damn it. Until the day had come when Fergus really did begin to sleep around, justifying himself by a simple argument which ran that if Sarah was so sure he was sleeping around he might as well actually do so; it would not make the situation worse than it was. So the cottage saw him less and less, till the day that Sarah announced she was going off to Rhodesia to join her lover, the much decorated, deeply conservative, veteran of the desert war who had inherited a farm near the Victoria Falls. A year later she announced that she was pregnant and wanted a divorce for the sake of the child; which her father managed cleanly, expeditiously.

Meanwhile Fergus learned his trade and began slowly to establish a reputation as a documentary film-maker. What he developed – made his own so that his peers (and the critics) came gradually to recognize it as his mark – was an unwavering gaze that challenged the audience to make a choice: to share that gaze, to turn to another channel or switch off. His detractors accused him of aestheticizing misery; others of voyeurism – a kind of pornography of suffering; others again were more dismissive saying that his slow style was a boring indulgence; but above his desk was pinned a cutting that read: 'Fergus MacIver's work is an unrelenting look at the misery of the world which, once he has made us see it, will not let us rest,' of which he was proud while publicly dismissing it as 'Pure pseud's corner'.

What he recorded was the unremitting labour of men and women and children in countries where the budget of one of his films could have fed a whole village for a year, got them a stand-pipe, had their babies innoculated. He worked always with the same cameraman whose unwavering gaze watched Indian women, the end of their saris wrapped round their faces against the red dust, labour all day carrying loads of bricks from the kilns. In a thronged street he returned obsessively to single out with a long lens the rickshaw boys who could not hope to live beyond thirty, or observed tenderly from far off the frail beauty of children playing by the open sewers. With him Fergus went on to record the grief of women as they rocked in mourning over the barefooted, bruised, lacerated, blood-caked corpses of husbands, brothers, sons, lovers in the Gaza Strip, the Lebanon, Chile, Nicaragua, San Salvador. With time a great anger built up inside him. It was fuelled by the images he had compiled and carried unbearably in his head.

With it went a sense of impotence, a feeling that there was no possible answer to the power of the men he had interviewed in their cool gleaming palaces of glass where they pursued policies that were logical, relentless, destructive of human life and the human environment. Or of the politicians, slippery debaters, who appealed to democracy, the values of the West, the free market, and in secret funded murderous attacks on those who out of their misery and despair dared to oppose them.

He did not consider himself a political person. After the sentimental Communism of his youth he had become a passive Labour supporter, content to accept the Welfare State and the slogan of Fair Shares For All. But through the lens of the camera and from the little screen of the cutting-room he had come to understand the lack of hope that drove men and women to believe that terrorism or armed uprising was the only possible response to the crushing weight of injustice. As he worked his anger mounted, but he knew no way of expressing it politically so he kept it to himself, consoling himself that to some degree, even if only minimally, his films were perhaps a blow struck at the oppressors of this world.

In a viewing theatre one day, looking at rushes from Northern Ireland – children of the slums banging their dustbin lids while the army's footpatrols danced their twirling ballet through the streets – he was introduced to a woman called Gordon. In her thirties, he guessed, dark, Jewish-looking, with a great track-record as a researcher, a linguist with Spanish connections, married to an ace cameraman. She joined his team. When her husband died in a helicopter that crashed into a wall of rock in the Alps, he comforted her, was solicitous, but respected her grief. They were close. Good friends. Good partners – nothing more. For a time at least.

In the course of these years he had acquired a reputation but few friends. Some of those few who held a shielding hand over him – as it were – began to tell him that at the highest levels in the Corporation where such things were discussed (but not necessarily minuted) people were beginning to say that they could only 'afford' a limited number of his kind of documentary, ones that raised questions. Interesting work, of course, that the BBC had a duty to present to the audience as a public service – but some of the Governors found his approach rather unbalanced. There had been mutterings, for instance, from a certain High Commissioner about one of MacIver's latest efforts which had made absolutely no attempt to put the problems of the Third World in perspective or to give an idea of the very considerable efforts the government of that country were making to combat poverty and disease. Not that MacIver's work wasn't very prestigious, and indeed had won its category at the Italia Prize. But there were other considerations and his head of department really ought to try to keep them in mind. Which was not to be read by anyone as the Corporation yielding to pressure – merely being realistic in the present political climate.

He was at this time unattached. Too busy to bother about relationships. Taking sex where he found it without commitment. Then at a party he found himself challenged about the politics of documentary film-making by a woman in her early thirties, small, plump, round-faced, blue-eyed, with an intelligence that flashed out from behind her beauty like a hidden weapon. He was drawn to her by a kind of excitement, an overwhelming curiosity. So he found himself in bed with Siobhan. And through her he came to the Party because – as she put it to him – there wasn't much point, was there, in his just going round the Third World filming starving kids, shanty towns, poverty and disease, not to mention the work of killers funded by the CIA – what for? To wring the hearts of the middle-classes and get good notices in the Sundays? Then doing nothing about it. Nothing political. All right, he was angry – which maybe made him feel better. But what good did that do anyone? 'Fergus,' she had said, sitting up in bed, pink and white, 'you've got to come and talk to Comrade Fred. We could use someone like you. We've all – all of us cultural workers – got to make up our minds whose side we're on. You can't be a fucking liberal all your life. There are other things than credit-titles and the rat-race. And you know it. All right. So do something about it.'

It was, he supposed, her experience as an actress used to stripping off on stage that made her walk so unselfconsciously naked across the room to peer through the slats of the blind, still talking, deciding how to arrange the meeting with Comrade Fred. She knew she could fix it. Comrade Fred would know who Fergus was. There were things Fergus could do for the movement. Then 'Shit,' she said, 'there's the au pair coming back from school with the kids. We'd better get dressed.'

Siobhan had to vouch for him to a middle-aged man in overalls before Fergus could pass through the big blind gate of the Boatyard for the first time. Once inside she guided him down a long bare corridor with windows on the canal side that were carefully screened with white paint; at the end she knocked at an office door. It was opened by a young woman with a curious habit of glancing downwards as if afraid of meeting Fergus's eyes. Silently she motioned him in and disappeared to join Siobhan in the corridor.

Comrade Fred, rather small, conventionally dressed, in his sixties with greying hair cut *en brosse*, rose from behind his desk to take his hand in a firm grip. 'Come away in, Mr MacIver. I hear you're angry about something. That's always a beginning.' They could speak freely, he assured Fergus with an unexpected boyish grin; the office had been debugged. 'I've been too long in the game to be caught out like that. An old fox, you might say.' From a drawer he produced a tiny gadget that looked as if it might be some sort of microphone and quickly put it away again. 'You know where it was? In a light fixture. But we found it, we found it. We don't play around.'

It had been, Fergus thought when he emerged, an extra-ordinary conversation – in part an interrogation, in part a detailed analysis that ranged from the Labour Party and its relationship to the TUC to the situation in Chile. He had to admit that it made a lot of sense. There were other passages which he found more obscure; they concerned doctrinal differences with comrades in the States and elsewhere who were denounced with passion. Underlying it all was a critique of the Soviet system as a distorted workers' state which he had heard before from Siobhan and felt some doubts about, but he wasn't prepared to argue. What had surprised him most of all was the reference to his ex-father-in-law.

'Frank Hewson, now, your ex-father-in-law – you see we're well-informed – with his chambers in Cliffords Inn. QC. Unlucky not to have made it to the bench. Sharp though. Nearly had me sent down once. For incitement to mutiny. But my man was better than him. They couldn't make it stick.' Comrade Fred rubbed his hands and once again the grin spread over his face. 'Handles security cases for the Crown. A reactionary bastard, if you don't mind me saying so. But we'll deal with the likes of him. You remember the Peasants' Revolt and what they did to the judges and lawyers. Cut their heads off. And quite right too. Class war is a tough business, comrade.'

What Fergus found himself committed to was attendance

at a group – he'd find a lot of mates there, he'd be surprised. And indeed he did find several known faces from television when he turned up at his first meeting in Comrade Siobhan's flat and immediately found himself involved in Party activities – putting together (under an assumed name) a documentary for Party purposes on the struggle in Central America. It was a step with consequences he had not anticipated but which he now accepted as inevitable. When he began to speak at Party meetings, to give showings of his films, to stand for office in the union on the Party ticket, he found his head of department no longer gave him his head as a sharp-eyed observer of oppression and exploitation whose work though radical could be tolerated because it looked good in the Annual Report; instead, under cover of a departmental rejigging he found himself marginalized.

So there began a period of depression in which he turned increasingly not to the Wise Woman with her consulting room that gave on to a Hampstead square but to Judith, from whom he increasingly got support of a different kind. In the warmth of her bed she comforted him, nursed him almost and for the first time since Kevin crashed to his death in the Alps entered into a relationship. So they became lovers and from being lovers, partners – a pair and recognized as such.

When (to her mother's satisfaction) Judith abandoned the remoteness of Lavender Hill and at last came 'North of the River', Fergus moved with her into a basement flat in Highbury. Judith set about nursing the garden into colour, sited shrubs, the ceanothus, the jasmine, the honeysuckle, and planted clusters of herbs by the French window. Lying in bed they looked out on to a long lawn which – by default on the part of transient tenants in the flats above – was almost her preserve. At its far end were poplars like tall green cockades and an amazingly high pear-tree, that sent a blizzard of petals across the lawn in spring, and in summer was full of blackbirds and jays, of squirrels which let fall through the foliage half-eaten fruit that plopped on to the ground to rot among the long grass at its base.

By the time the pears were falling for the second time, their honeymoon days were over. Now Fergus spent hours in the garden, savaging a bed of nettles, lopping a fallen apple-tree, giving vent to anger and frustration at his lack of employment. It was a state of idleness which he countered by allowing himself to be drawn more and more into political work. But politics had to be extra-mural, as it were, for the flat was unequivocally – and not only in terms of the title-deeds – Judith's territory. It followed that Fergus was never allowed to use it for meetings of 'the comrades', whom she kept at bay as surely as if there were a magic fence round the flat, which they could only penetrate (as they did too often for her liking) by telephone, by letter, by summons to this meeting or that, by instructions to be at six prompt (in the morning) at King's Cross to pick up the papers along with a comrade (Siobhan?) and distribute them over half of North London, to attend a meeting in Siobhan's flat. When Siobhan was photographed in that same flat for a colour supplement, and the accompanying article spoke of her friendship with a famous stage-designer, Judith's sexual jealousy was somewhat allayed but it was replaced by a sense of neglect. This she laid at the door of the Boatyard, from which she was physically excluded and on which her resentments were increasingly focused.

The day that Fergus returned to say that he had managed to get a commission for a documentary on the Indian State railways the burden of anomie visibly lifted from him. Just think, he said, what fun it would be to shoot all these wonderful coal and wood-burning locos crossing the Ghats or whatever those hills in the Deccan were called. She objected that it didn't exactly sound like his scene but he laughed and hugged her. He wanted to do something not about out-of-date technology – although mind you the engines were splendid – but about the railway system of the Indian subcontinent. To use its great obsolescent engines as a symbol of the strength of the Indian working-class. He could see the shots already.

Months later, viewing the rushes, she did indeed see these huge locomotives, powerful, waiting like great hump-backed animals, wreathed in steam, in the chill of the dawn, while the men who mastered them, frail beneath the towering bulk of the engines, picked their way over the criss-crossing rails and points; the men who had mounted an all-out strike and challenged the Congress Party and its corrupt leadership.

Saw, too, how in shot after shot the symbolism of the locomotive imposed itself on the viewer. Intercut were interviews with slim, soft-spoken men who talked of their lives, their determination to fight, the power of their common cause. Judith was aware that as they watched the tall, thin sardonic man who was Fergus's producer was shifting uneasily in his seat. She put her hand out to find Fergus's. The lights went up. No one said anything. Then, without turning round, the man said in his dry, level voice: 'You can't stop banging your Marxist drum, can you? This is going to drop me in the shit again. You do see that, don't you? Jesus, we try to protect you but what's the use?' The film was never made, although some of the footage eventually turned up in a travelogue about India.

Once more Fergus despaired.

His depression barely lifted when the same editor rang to say he wanted to have a chat. 'Chat', in institutional language, was a dangerous word. So in an office cluttered with diplomas, festival trophies, awards of one kind and another, they chatted about things they had seen on the box recently, a smokescreen of acute exchanges that obscured the real point of the meeting, which the editor suddenly revealed, altering the nature of their exchange – as Fergus told Judith – like a sudden change of gear. As a great favour and because he had an immense respect for what Fergus had done in the past, the editor was going to offer him the chance to direct one of a prestigious historical series called 'Perspectives'.

It was a project Fergus knew well, one for which safe academics provided a balanced commentary. In filmic terms it had, in his judgement, contrived to reduce the slave trade to beautiful shots of the beaches of West Africa, to bows shearing the water while the voice over recounted the horrors of the Middle Passage. He recalled – as no doubt the editor did – his saying at a departmental meeting, that what the viewer was left with was not (how could it be?) the stench of shit and vomit and death between decks where the slaves lay in irons, head to foot, men, women and children, but the effortless grace of the porpoises that paced the ship. What the editor was now offering was a programme on the Peninsular War – great stuff – what did Wellington say about his troops, something like 'I don't know about the enemy but by God they frighten me'? – and of course the Spanish guerillas, Goya's horrors of war. Strong visual material and no doubt Fergus would find a radical slant. Maybe when he was in Madrid he could have a shot at setting up a co-production with Spanish television. Worth a try. In any case, in spite of Fergus's criticisms – and maybe there was something to them – the programme on the slave trade had gone down very well indeed with an independent public service station in Boston or was it Connecticut? The meeting was all very chummy and jokey, but what was clear to Fergus was that as far as the offer went he could take it or leave it; that this was a last chance. So Judith got a new notebook, labelled it Penwar and began her patient work of drawing up a bibliography, searching for contemporary prints, planning itineraries.

Now as he stood by the window where his breath condensed on the cold glass, Fergus was aware of a distance between himself and Judith that no word or gesture of his could cross. On her return she had lain down on the bed and was perhaps sleeping, perhaps merely avoiding looking at him, talking to him, engaging with him in any way. He looked at his watch. It was barely two o'clock. A desert of time stretched before them till night. As often in other circumstances – waiting while some official decided whether the bribe he had been offered was big enough to cause him to grant permission for Fergus to shoot on some normally forbidden location, listening for his bedside phone to ring and a voice to propose a rendezvous that might be more or less clandestine, more or less dangerous – he too sought sleep as the only way to kill time; which was, he thought as he began to doze, an odd way of putting it. After all time would certainly in the long run have its revenge.

He was wakened by a knock. In a confused moment he called out 'Entrez!' and jumped to his feet. It was the maid, noiseless in her soft slippers. Mutely she held out a folded piece of paper and, turning on her heel, left the room. In the half-light from the drawn curtain he could make out a couple of lines in childish capitals. He slithered on a rug as he ran towards the door and had to steady himself for a second against the table. The corridor was empty. The maid had vanished down some backstairs or through an unmarked door. Judith was sitting up. He held the paper out to her. *El Hogar 2200 cochinillo asado. Un amigo de Carlos.*

'Well,' he said.

'You have an appointment at eight o'clock at this restaurant. You should order roast sucking pig. It's a local delicacy.'

'I had better go.'

'Are you going to tell me what this is all about?' she asked.

'Sometimes the less people know the better.'

'But you still want me to come.'

'I'd be grateful.'

Fergus watched the porter's face as he gave Judith directions on how to find the restaurant, but there was no obvious significance in his insistence that they must try the *cochinillo asado*. As they passed under the aqueduct he was touched to feel her hand on his arm, but that could not bridge the gap between thoughts that both were aware of as silences. In the inner pocket of his raincoat Fergus felt the passport he had extracted from the lining of his camera case. It would be no great deal, a matter of handing it over unobtrusively and then back to the hotel. Tomorrow, he assured Judith, they would turn south towards Albacete, where the volunteers of the International Brigades had climbed onto the trucks that brought them in long convoys to the front, and if she really wanted it, to the valley of the Jarama. Though for the life of him he couldn't see what she expected to get out of her pilgrimage to either place, what insight into the end of a father whose grave was as anonymous and unknown as those of the men who had come from the English counties or from the Highlands and Islands to fight in the Peninsula nearly two hundred years before.

What Judith thought in her silence was presumably more complicated, for she lacked the simple certainties that seemed to lie behind Fergus's actions and decisions. She carried with her memories of exchanges in a warm room with subdued lighting, in which a man with the clipped South African accent had listened to her carefully, attentively, interjecting an occasional question to which she replied as truthfully as she could find it in her to do: questions that suggested that her anger was fruitless and would turn to a bitterness every whit as destructive as her mother's cherished resentments; that she would do better to try to reach down into herself for a sense of forgiveness. That only by some sort of inner reconciliation with the dead man would she be able to stop searching for other men with the authority and power to replace the one she had lost. It was a proposition which she resisted and was prepared to reject, challenging the way the ancient Oedipal myth was being imposed on her. But for the moment there was this ridiculous errand to be accomplished. Later, when they got back to London, she would have things out with Fergus, who would no doubt fight back with all his power and his knowledge of her fears and weaknesses. But this time she was determined to win.

The restaurant: more or less empty, old-fashioned. Plainly furnished, the mirrors on the walls tarnished in their gilt frames, the images they returned uncertain and imprecise; above the bar the waxen portrait of the man who lay dying in Madrid. It was an everyday place, slightly worn, a little shabby. Fergus knew such undramatic settings – bars, hotel foyers, restaurants, cafés – where he had made rendezvous with men of violence, men of power, men heroic in their defiance of tyranny and men whose one aim was revenge, vendetta, men who would risk their lives for money and were indifferent whom they served, agents and double-agents, eager to use him for their own ends, dangerous, tricky, smooth, threatening, but prepared to meet, to talk, to discuss, to make propositions, to volunteer some crumb of information or to plant some lie in spots like this – in Ulster, in the Lebanon, in Caracas – where the proprietors and the waiters either were unaware of what passed between their clients or feigned ignorance, asking no questions and being told no lies. So he was not surprised at the nonchalance with which the proprietor indicated a table and gestured to the young waiter who leant against the bar to attend to them.

The waiter was tall, dark, in his twenties. Deft, quick to compliment Judith when she ordered in Spanish. *Entremeses* – and did they have *cochinillo asado – agua mineral – sin gaz? Otra cosa?* he asked. *Vino?* Fergus nodded impatiently. *Rojo?* They waited. The other customers looked like regulars – bachelors, teachers, civil servants or bank clerks perhaps, who came each evening to eat their dinners in silence, exchanging few words with the waiters, uninterested in the foreign couple, intent on a newspaper or book, measuring out their wine from bottles that bore on their labels a mark of ownership. Judith wondered whether her poet had sat there alone, after death had come on that summer evening.

The meal was adequate. The pork tender. The wine tangy, a little rough. Fergus had the inevitable egg-custard and wondered why the Spaniards insisted on calling it 'flan'; Judith could offer no explanation and made it clear she was not interested in discussing the conundrum. Having picked at her food she now asked only for fruit.

After coffee they sat and wondered what next to do. The waiter refused to let Fergus catch his eye and kept wandering to the door where the coats hung. At last Fergus managed to attract his attention and call for the bill. Fergus paid. When the waiter, slow in returning after a consultation at the bar, presented the change Fergus refused it with a gesture of annoyance. The young man swept up the change and then surprisingly lingered and became suddenly talkative. Were they Americans? From London? He had been in London. He had a friend there, a student called Carlos. Did they know Carlos? London was a big place, said Judith, looking sharply at Fergus at the mention of the name. The waiter smiled and agreed. He had not been there for a while. At the door he was assiduous in helping Fergus on with his coat, setting the belt right, careful to adjust his raincoat collar because, as he explained, it was going to rain again – autumn weather. At the door he bowed and thanked them, wished them a very good evening and they were out on the street where they stood for a second with the rain spitting on the flagged pavement. They turned and walked down the hill. The noise of their footsteps sounded inordinately loud in the empty street. Once in their room Fergus felt in his inside pocket. It was empty. Judith asked whether he was sure. Sure of what? Sure it was all right. As sure as he could be, Fergus replied. She could see how easy it had been. Tomorrow they would be on their way.

They made love that night – if that was the right expression for holding and touching that had more to do with memory, custom, habit, reflex responses and the easing of tensions, than with anything Judith could equate with love. But perhaps this was all love was: the feel of an arm round her as she fell asleep, the sensation of another body, warm and close in the night and at waking: the comforts of the cave, of the igloo and the hut.

In the room the nun on duty was older than the one the night before. In her sixties, she remembered the Civil War, the burning churches, the mummified bodies of the nuns exposed in the streets of Barcelona, the hatred – inexplicable to her – that had exploded throughout her country against the religion of her order. She had lived in its shelter since she was a girl when, in a terrible act of rebellion, she had escaped into the safety of the convent from her father, the atheistical, radical provincial lawyer who had mocked her mother's simple piety and her own adolescent longings for a vocation. She was hard in her faith, hard in her need for revenge, grateful for the man whose last moments she was watching over, fearful for what would come once they allowed him to die. She was a devotee of the Eternal Rosary and her hour was two in the morning. She was used to waken then and to add her voice to the thousands of voices all over the Catholic world hailing the maid full of grace who had been in her turn conceived without sin, a bride chosen by God as, in a more humble way, the nun herself was a bride of Christ.

As she waited for her hour in the Rosary to come she listened to the breathing of the man who had led the crusade against the evils of Marxism and freemasonry, of anarchism, of atheists like her father for whom, she knew with deep sadness, her prayers could do nothing. So if the man whose last hours she was witnessing had to punish with death the criminals and heretics of the war, she thought of it as a process of purging and comforted herself with the thought that no doubt many of them at the last moment – or so she had heard – had found consolation in the ministry of the prison chaplains and might hope for salvation and the remission of their grievous sins. She often specially remembered those penitents in her prayers.

A rattle of rain on the window wakened Fergus to the warmth of the bed he shared. It was a warmth that he found deeply reassuring. He was relieved. There had been no hitch. Mission accomplished. They could turn back to battlefields of the Peninsula: Vimiero, Bussaco, Talavera, Fuentes de Oñoro, Vittoria. As often, he found himself thinking of the men (and their women – sixty to a battalion) marching on foot, on horse, in carts, sometimes barefoot, through the dust of the interminable dry summer roads or the mud of the autumn and winter, across the sierras and over the great plateau of Castille. He wondered what had brought them there. Poverty, of course. Hunger. Like that man from an Irish regiment, the Connaught Rangers – Judith had discovered him in a book of memoirs – who called himself 'an Irish fellow who has been accustomed all his life to be what an Englishman would consider half-starved.' But beyond that, in some cases at least, a desperate need to escape: from cramped lives, from hardships, from ties – family ties, ties of kinship, of community.

His father used to tell a story – but perhaps it was no more than a vague memory passed down and embroidered over the generations – of two men on *his* father's side, sturdy itinerant cobblers ('soutars' he called them, in the dialect of his youth), who, leaving the braes of Balquhidder, had listed in the Argylls and been lost in Spain. Had theirs

60

been merely a roving impulse or did there lie behind it the desire to know whether they could face the moment of action – that moment Fergus himself had watched but only from the margin of the fight, from a distance, never having to stand and endure it. Not like that Irishman or the men in the Argyll and Sutherland Highlanders driven from their land by sheep in the Highland Clearances, little better than mercenaries but buoyed up – by what? – by hatred of the Frenchies, by slogans about King and Country, by legends about Old Boney who ate children?

Yet these were the men who had lain patiently on the reverse slope of a hill-top in Portugal and waited. Then at a shouted command they rose up in their triple ranks, saw the French storming up hill but must hold their fire till their volleys could blow away the head of the attacking column. Engulfed in the thick choking smoke of their musketry, which clung to their clothes and so blinded them that they saw only the flash of their muskets, they heard the hiss and hum of cannon-balls, the thud as they fell among their own ranks, the cries of the wounded and the shouts of the officers to close up and fill the gaps.

He could understand better those like Judith's father who had volunteered for a principle, for a cause that had drawn them across the frontiers, from Germany, Austria, Poland, Italy and even the United States, just as they had been drawn from South Wales, London and Fife. These were men he had to respect, although they had been mostly – in the case of Judith's father certainly – Stalinists whose generosity Stalin had used for his own ends and then abandoned, just as he abandoned the Spanish Republic. But at least they had been fighting Fascism on grounds of political commitment, seeing clearly that their war was likely to be the prologue to a vaster struggle.

But he had a suspicion derived from memoirs, from diaries, from accounts here and there, that some of those men, too, had been taken by the lure of war – the sharp taste of excitement, the deep unconfessable desire to feel the razor-edge of fear. He knew that desire and (having once been thwarted) had contrived in his chosen profession to put himself in situations where he had heard the crack of air-burst shells, the whoosh of mortar bombs, the crackle of rifle-fire. So he had been frightened. But not to the very limits. Frightened for his life. But not in duty bound to hazard it the lottery of battle. For he could at any time retire, take cover, retreat without shame, and need not stand up and walk over ground where the machine-gun bullets threw up gravel and earth and tufts of grass.

As he lay with open eyes in the dark, and things began to assume shape and outlines, he could see his hand lying on the cover of the bed where it had come to rest in sleep. He flexed the fingers a little and wondered whether the man who lay dying in Madrid was at times aware through half-open eyes of the bed in which he lay, whether he knew he was dying and whether he was capable of fear. Perhaps he had passed beyond that point and was in some state suspended between perception and oblivion. But what did that mean, 'oblivion'? One was oblivious in sleep, or under an anaesthetic, and yet somehow somewhere sentient, a functioning organism, living protein – to put it no higher. So that if he thought of the dying man he could imagine that his hand, which perhaps lay on the coverlet as his own did, might conceivably give a slight movement, a twitch of a muscle that was like a twinge of memory. Of the way his fingers used to grip the stock of his hunting rifle in the high Pyrenees with a chamois in his sights, when a strong even pressure on the trigger would bring the animal tumbling down over the rocks. Or a flexing of the muscles as when he stretched fingers cramped from the signing of official documents. Decrees, commissions, letters to dignitaries of the church, to heads of government, replies to requests for a pension, for a pardon to be extended to some young man of good family (devout Catholics, a brother in the priesthood) who had in a foolish moment thrown his youth and energy into the lost Republican cause, to all of which he replied or had replies written out of a deep sense of duty – the same duty as guided his fingers when he signed the sheaves of death sentences that came each afternoon from the tribunals: because justice had to be done and rebellion stamped out for a generation at least. Documents where the worst cases were flagged and on which he might add in his careful hand: Death by garotte – death by garotte with dishonour – death by garotte with press presence.

The priest who had spied for the French, wrote the rifleman who saw it all in Madrid's Plaza Mayor, *wanted to address the people but was prevented. His arms were then bound with cords and the iron collar was placed upon his throat. Women who waved their handkerchiefs with joy upon his arrival at the scaffold now might be seen closing their eyes or wiping away a tear. One of the priests read from a book and the other heard the spy's last words. When he had finished reading he stooped down to kiss the ill-fated man's cheek. A cloth was thrown over the man's face; the executioner turned the screw and he was dead.*

The nun had seen the slight retraction of the muscles and had slipped into the hand – it was still warm to the touch – a rosary from the table by the bedside, plain, fashioned they said from an olive tree on Gethsemane, blessed by a prince of the Church, perhaps even by the Holy Father. The fingers retracted again as if to grasp it but once more lost tension and the rosary slipped down over the coverlet. The nun gathered it, raised it to her lips. As she did so she heard a noise in the man's throat, a rattle, the result of a great effort, a strange noise that died away into a silence in which she heard his voice, painfully, slowly, but clearly say: 'How hard it is to die.' Then silence, a sharp intake of the breath, and the breathing settled back into its rhythm. She began to pray.

63

In his room Fergus turned in his bed and fitted himself against Judith's back. His right arm encircled her and his hand moved down to allow itself to be imprisoned between her thighs. Then in safety he slept again. Safe. Safe from the fear of death that had used to make him as a child sit up in terror in the dark and, as he thought now of the dying tyrant, had seeped back into his consciousness.

Judith was the first to wake. She moved gently in the bed and lifted the weight of Fergus's arm from her body. She had a feeling that their lovemaking had been a step backwards rather than forwards, that it would make it the more difficult to discuss the how and the why of their relationship, its permanence, its duration, its purpose, its usefulness to either of them. Now she felt she must imagine them returning to her basement flat but beyond that she saw herself alone, coming to terms with herself, defining herself in the present and not in terms of the past, contemplating a future that might in some ways be lonely but one in which she was not a name in a credit sequence of yet another documentary by Fergus MacIver. And she braced herself in advance to withstand his tears, his childish anger, his despair, which she could assuage only by sacrifices she was no longer prepared to make. He would try everything – down to massaging the nape of her neck, which as both very well knew was a source of tingling pleasure to her. But she would deny him. Would – for a space at least – give up sex, concentrate on her possible future as a director. In a year or so she might risk it again, but picking and choosing. There were, after all, a lot of nice men in the world with whom she would not mind mutual exploration, mutual pleasure. But no commitments. Definitely no commitments.

She got up and ventured across the cold tiled floor. On her way back from the shower cubicle in the corner of the room she noticed a folded piece of paper on the floor by the door. It had not been there when she rose. When she stooped to pick it up she recognized it as the same faintly ruled paper as had been used to set up the appointment the day before. *Tengo que verte. Los Huertos. En la iglesia. A la una. Importante. Urgente. Un amigo de Carlos.* She drew her dressing-gown more tightly round her; if she shivered slightly, it was less because of cold than of a moment of panic. She stuffed the paper into her dressing-gown pocket and sitting before the mirror began to brush her hair, slowly, reflectively. It was a ritual that gave her time to decide how to confront the situation. The alternatives were simple. Either she told Fergus that 'a friend of Carlos' – but how many friends did Carlos have? and who were they and were they what they said they were? – wanted Fergus to make contact in some village church at midday, or she quite simply flushed the paper down the loo. After all, if Fergus had been telling the truth – but had he? – the mission he had undertaken had been accomplished. So there was no earthly reason for them to hang on.

She felt a sudden access of annoyance – more – of anger at her dependence on this man who lay there still drowsing. Even if she somehow made her way to Madrid alone – she was strongly tempted to try it – she would have to wait there, for they had Apex tickets and there was no way in which she could take an earlier flight from Madrid. That meant a wait of five days. What tugged in the other direction was her deep desire to avoid the kind of dishonesty of which she knew Fergus to be capable: in terms of fibs, half-truths (about that cow Siobhan), the stratagems by which, in her experience, men rationalized their behaviour, attempted to conceal their infidelities, soothed and deceived their partners, lovers, wives. For men, experience had taught her, are by nature duplicitous, It was in some important way necessary as a woman to be truthful and face the consequences.

Fergus sat up in bed, shivered and pulled the clothes round himself. 'Hi,' he said. 'Hi,' she replied and went on brushing her hair. She found him touching in the morning. His reddish hair, thinning now, tousled, his face pink with sleep. His lips soft and babyish. Found it comical how he shambled about the room, fishing for a piece of clothing in his travel-bag, humming in the shower. But she could not shield him for ever from the consequences of his choices. When he emerged, pinker than ever, from the shower and stood there rubbing his head with the towel, she had already laid the note on the table where he was bound to see it. As he did, picking it up and examining it. When had it come, he demanded to know. She said she wasn't sure. Did he understand what it said?

'Something about waiting for a friend of Carlos.'

'Well,' she said.

'Where's – what's it called – Los Huertos?'

'So you're going to meet him, whoever he is?'

'I've got to.'

'What d'you mean, got to?'

He reflected for a moment.

'I must – that's all there is to it.'

'What about me?'

He rubbed his head in silence. She could have struck him.

'What was all that last night then, about mission accomplished and so on?' When she was angry her face became pale and drawn as it was when she had her migraines. 'Why on earth have you got to go on playing this ridiculous game, and dragging me into it?'

'You don't begin to understand.'

'I want to go back to Madrid. Home.'

Calmly, infuriatingly, he demonstrated to her that for purely practical reasons they had to stick together, that the car down there in the courtyard was hired in his name and anyway she couldn't drive, hadn't managed to pass her test at the fourth attempt, that their tickets couldn't be changed, that they didn't have the cash to do it anyway and didn't she say she wanted to go to Albacete or the valley of the Jarama;

66

which was damnably unfair of him, she objected, as she sat and brushed her hair, dashing away a tear with an angry gesture. She finished dressing quickly and stuffed her things in her holdall. Picking up her bag, she left the room. Then re-opening the door she said: 'You're a lot of fucking Moonies and I think you're mad.'

In the corridor there was the maid in her soft shoes carrying a load of clean bed-linen. '*Buenas dias*,' she said. Judith returned the greeting automatically and passed on; but suddenly she turned and ran back to catch the young woman before she vanished into a laundry cupboard. The maid faced her calmly. In her twenties, broad-shouldered, peasant-looking, plain but with a good figure, she had a red birthmark splashed on the side of her neck just below her right ear. Had she put a note under the door, Judith demanded to know. The woman shrugged and wondered what the señora was talking about. She did her job, she said, if the señora was unhappy she should talk to the manager. And she went on calmly laying the linen on the shelves of the cupboard. Judith turned away angry and saddened. Just the kind of young woman, she thought, that Carlos and his friends would exploit – rather plain, flattered by their advances (which overlooked her birthmark), compromised, blackmailed, frightened by tough men, frightened for her job, frightened and submissive.

The morning dragged on. From the restaurant window Judith watched Fergus come and go, packing their things in the back of their hired car. Perhaps he had decided to be reasonable. She had an inescapable feeling that some sort of threshold had been crossed in their relationship. For her it had been what he said about going to Albacete and the Jarama, about that pilgrimage which was the true motive for her journey just as his was some crazy political mission.

Why, she wondered, did people who were partners deal their most deadly blows to each other with that terrible weapon – privileged knowledge of secret hopes and fears expressed in moments when body and mind, heart and feelings were at their most exposed. There had been similar crises between them – exchanges, silences, accusations, lies (on his part) not only about women but about his Party, which she had endured because of her dependence, emotional and professional, and because of her pride, her determination not to give her mother the satisfaction of welcoming her to the ranks of the regiment of deserted women. Now, though she lingered over her coffee and waited, she decided not to go in search of him, not to put out feelers, little hints, indications that might be no more than a smile or a funny face, an extended hand, a slight touch that could develop into a caress. She would accept the threshold of feeling, which would also be, she knew, if not now then later, a threshold of pain. So she stayed put.

When almost an hour had passed she once more walked past the desk and wondered whether there was a hidden significance in the way the porter greeted her. Was he, like the maid, a possible accomplice, the deliverer of notes, Fergus's fellow-conspirator, or was he a member of the secret police, a provocateur from the Seguridad – a word, a presence that had haunted the memories of the Republican exiles in Rome, the organization that had traced Sebastian's father on a mission to make contact with comrades from across the frontier. At Port Bou the French police had handed him over to stand trial in Franco's courts, so that one morning he walked out into a prison courtyard to be shot. There were times when she felt she knew more about the reality of politics under a dictatorship from the interminable discussions, the obsessively repeated stories of the Spanish exiles in Rome, than Fergus with all his correctly 'objective' analyses of the situation.

To kill time, to get through the long wait she must endure, she walked up through the town past the restaurant where the waiter bowed to her in recognition. The guide-book had spoken of a medieval merchant's house, had enumerated some of the town's 18 convents, its 73 churches and chapels, (not counting the cathedral, late Gothic), the Roman towers and gate of the municipal prison, the 170 arches of the aqueduct ('one of the most important pieces of Roman engineering in Spain'), but she was in no mood for antiquities. Instead she wandered through the town thinking of her poet and the loneliness that had attended him when he recalled '*your hand in mine, your friendly hand, your childish voice in my ear.*' Her aimless walk led her on past a building with walls pitted and scored by what she guessed was rifle and machine-gun fire from when the town was held against the Republicans. The Madonna, said her guidebook, had been designated a corps commander in the order of the day that celebrated the raising of the siege. From one of the seventy-three churches a bell began to ring for midday. So she turned back and once more she found her way past the restaurant where she was conscious of the waiter's gaze following her downhill – quizzically? But she must, she felt, control paranoia.

In front of the hotel Fergus was sitting in the driving seat, examining a map. He opened the door for her.

'It's only about half-an-hour's drive to the north. So it's no big deal.'

Judith made no comment as they drove off through hilly country where the villages, clumps of houses round little romanesque churches, huddled in hollows and the road with its sparse traffic switchbacked ahead of them. Normally she would have navigated with the map and their Guide Bleu on her knee, coping with the stress of long days of driving. Even before today – quite apart from the normal disputes about routes, mistakes in map-reading, differences about when and where to stop for the night – this had not been a happy trip. Fergus had been remote, edgy, preoccupied with matters he did not offer to share. On top of this he had been infuriated by the tact of the guidebook in dealing with the Civil War, its suppression of anything that might raise a disturbing memory or incite the imagination of a tourist by recalling that there had been a Republic, the trouble it took not to recall that in living memory this ridge they were driving over had been a contested height, that bridge an opposed river-crossing, an olive-grove ground once fought over, won, lost and retaken. She had tried to coax him out of his mood, to make him laugh by jokes about the categories used to define a town, a church, a castle, ranging from *important* through *vaut un détour* down to a mere *intéressant*. It was as *intéressant* that with a wave of the hand they came to dismiss some distant village with its 'baptismal font – C12' unvisited by them and (they suspected) by others.

Judith had a feeling that Los Huertos would turn out to be just such an obscure place, where in the afternoon all that would be stirring would be a dog and a few hens scratching in the dust. The church would be small, with a porch where stiff saints and angels surrounded an inexpressive God the Father, and among the vine tendrils that decorated the columns there might at best be some grotesque human or animal face. To visit Los Huertos people would need a purpose – like Fergus and herself or like the women who had followed the marching columns across the Peninsula and descended on such villages in search of some eggs, a piece of cheese or (a treasure) a piece of smoked *jamon*.

Often over the last days she had thought of those women, huddled in their carts in the rain or snow or walking alongside while the horses or oxen or mules strained uphill in the heat. If the men were ill-shod, patched, tattered, what would the garb of the women have been like? Did they sometimes wear finery saved from the pillage: clothing the men had taken from looted houses and dresses torn from the backs of the foreign women who were their victims? Decked out like that the women would not have been easily put down but bold and confident, like the gipsy women she had seen as a girl at the fair on Hampstead Heath; travellers like them, moved from one unknown destination to another, uncomprehending, knowing only vaguely that they were in Spain – wherever Spain might be – perhaps not knowing even that, not caring.

How, she wondered, had they coped with womanhood? Sex, presumably, had been the currency with which they paid for such favours as they received from the men: a tot of rum, a chicken, the lace from a priest's cope, a piece of tinsel snatched from the image of a saint or a Madonna at the sack of some convent. But what about pregnancy? Contraception – a matter of old wives' tales about moss and vinegar? Or women's secret skills? What about their periods – or had they stopped because of the hardships of the campaign, the unremitting physical effort, the exertion of foraging and cooking and pitching and striking camp? If they had children, how did they contrive to look after them, care for them, protect them? How many of the children they bore were buried in shallow graves beside the roads that led to battle? How many of the women themselves had died of illness, of infections, puerperal fever, malaria, dysentery, victims of sudden raids when the enemy cavalry fell on the baggage trains, of a chance shot or a stray cannonball that came bounding across the dry, hard plain and plunged among the waggons?

They must have formed a tough sisterhood that fatigue, danger and homesickness bonded to the point where they could lay down certain rules to govern their relations with the men they shared and who shared them. But their story was untold. All they rated was a mention, half-jocular, knowing, in some officer's diary, some rifleman's journal. They were inscribed almost illegibly in the margin of history, as she felt herself to be inscribed. But she had no sisters to comfort and support her now when she felt helpless, at the whim of powers over which she had no control.

Los Huertos was as she had imagined it. It lay half a mile off the main road. A square. Brown houses. No one in the street. The church was near the entrance to the village. Small, squat, uninteresting. Fergus stopped the car close to the steps. There was no one waiting. Judith hesitated when he got out of the car and went slowly up the steps, pretending to examine the sculptures and the great bronze handle on the door with its grotesque gorgon-like face. But she felt exposed sitting alone in the front seat and quickly followed him. The interior was dark. She could make out an iron rack for the votive candles, the font, and everywhere the symbol that had presided over the auto-da-fés in which Jews had been tortured, garroted, burned: the elaborate crucifix behind the high altar, the stations of the cross on the walls, the repugnant symbols of masochism and cruelty. Fergus walked slowly ahead of her towards the altar-rail. The place seemed empty. As he turned and retraced his steps towards her she saw a figure emerge from the confessional halfway down the north aisle. A priest, she thought, but it was a young man with a pale drawn face like a mannerist saint who said in passable English that he was a friend of Carlos. In his hand he carried a small suitcase. He handed it to Fergus together with a piece of paper. 'The address,' he said, 'the comrades expect you tonight. Salud!' Then he slipped back into the shadow.

Outside there was thin sunlight. Fergus laid the suitcase on the back seat and they drove off. Their route took them back through the town where they had stayed, past their hotel, under the aqueduct and on towards Madrid. Judith was silent. She had turned her head a couple of times to look at the suitcase, which was cheap and slightly worn: the suitcase of a country student on his way to university or of a maid going to her first job in the city, not one that might plausibly belong to Fergus or herself. At length she laid her hand on Fergus's arm and asked him to stop. He said okay, when he got to a reasonable place, he couldn't just stop in the middle of the road. It seemed an interminable time till at last he turned off into a secondary road, parked and got out.

'We can't hang about,' he said, standing in the open door, 'I've got to find this address.'

'I think we should dump it. Get a hotel and then push on.'

He was peeing like a small boy, concentrating seriously on the way his urine made a puddle in the roadside dust. Like a boy, too, in the mulish look he had as he shook his head at her suggestion. It was a trait she had once found endearing, slightly ridiculous, the cue for affectionate teasing. Now it angered her.

'Have you any idea what's in that thing?' she asked.

He shrugged.

'Literature maybe. Leaflets. Stickers.'

'Suppose it's explosives,' she said, 'a bomb.'

'Don't be silly. The comrades would have warned me. You're just being hysterical.'

She said nothing but leant over to the back seat and took the suitcase. He tried to stop her but she turned away from him and tried the lock. It was securely shut. She laid the suitcase on his lap.

'Sometimes you are such a baby. At least have the sense to put it in the boot. Better still. Inside your big bag, if it will go.'

Reluctantly he agreed.

'Right,' he said as he banged down the lid of the boot, 'we're on our way.'

They had not driven far before he saw that she was sleeping.

Sleep is a refuge. But it is also — or can be — as aggressive as a silence, a way of being mute out of malice like a reluctant witness, the offence they used to punish by crushing the victim beneath a load of weights: the peine forte et dure. *Faced with it, we are tempted to lay on our sleeping partner the deadly weight of our resentments, the load of our unconfessed anger and suppressed hatred.*

Judith was an expert sleeper, for sleep had been her mode of escape from migraines, from her mother, from her desolation, from her grief when Kev was killed. But she had learned that she could be punished for her evasion. Fergus had great skills in this line.

The car was running well. A tinny noise from the exhaust that had annoyed Fergus a couple of days before seemed to have stopped. The road switchbacked over the Sierra and then began to fall through hairpin bends to the plateau that held the capital, the city that had stood out against the four attacking columns of the rebellious army whose commander now lay dying there. It was beginning to grow dark. The doctors – there would be an array of them in masks and aprons, in tailcoats and clothing that was already almost mourning – he could imagine thronging the antechambers, only the most favoured and most trusted allowed to penetrate to the inner room to check the breathing, the flutter of the pulse, the irregular beat of the obstinate heart. Outside, in little conclaves, the courtiers would be consulting, speculating, exchanging rumours, weighing up their situation, wondering where to turn to find some man, some political force, to which they might safely switch their allegiance. For they knew that the ultimate decision to disconnect the pipes and instruments, the elaborate support system, that kept the great man alive, would depend not on professional judgement but on a political calculation that would justify the ending of his life. Among them were soldiers with medal ribbons and sashes, prelates in birettas, tonsured monks and friars, wimpled nuns and starched nursing sisters, uniformed members of the Falange whose *jefe* he had been, dark-suited politicians and government officials, technocrats of Opus Dei, discreet and devout, concealing under their pious concern hopes for a modern capitalist state and beneath their sober suits the devices with which they mortified the flesh. Somewhere, in some inner room, was the family, no doubt enjoying the consolations of religion, waiting to be summoned to witness an event that could not with decency be delayed much longer, one that would call forth official manifestations of grief and secret rejoicings. It was as if the body of the dead man were suspended over the capital and the country, a presence as terrible as the phantasms that floated through his mind when the brain flickered for an instant into some sort of consciousness.

Fergus let her sleep. He knew the road, knew that he had a couple of hours to drive, knew that to the right lay the Valley of the Fallen and that later he would see the turn off to the Escorial where King Philip had arranged things so that from his bed he might see the altar and even when he lay dying assist at the rites of the Mass in the chill of that austere monument to the cult of renunciation and death. It would not be till they reached the suburbs that he would have to waken her and puzzle out from their town-plan of Madrid where the address was that he must reach that night. He felt alert – not strung up but very aware of the line of the road, the exact curve of the bend, the outline of the hills to his right, the lights, very far off, of some pueblo and, even further off beyond the distant horizon, a vague luminance rising into the sky that was presumably Madrid.

He went over again the possible snags that lay ahead. There might be road-blocks. The army, the police or the Guardia Civil might be stopping and searching cars entering the capital. He would rely on a British passport and that rigmarole about letting him pass without let or hindrance. But he must warn Judith not to speak Spanish; it would be more useful if she could simply listen and tell him what was being said. Only if things got really sticky might she admit to some rudimentary knowledge of the language. If the worst came to the worst, they could try what his father had used to call 'playing the daft laddie' – innocents abroad on whom a suitcase had been foisted about which they knew nothing. He hoped Judith would go along with the plan. She didn't have many alternatives and in any case, whatever the resentments she nursed, she was hardly likely to betray him. There was always the danger that, if the Seguridad were half as good as she sometimes indicated, she might be on their files from her time in Rome and with Sebastian. But that was a minor worry.

His real concern he had not confessed to her. It was that she might be right. The whole thing might be an elaborate frame-up. Carlos might have been arrested, might have talked. The 'friend of Carlos' might quite simply be a pro-vocateur. If so, the trap was set. He could only trust his luck, take a chance. Press on and see. He had done this sort of thing in half-a-dozen countries where people had dis-appeared, been kidnapped, found shot and mutilated. He recognized once more the tingling excitement laced with fear that was like a shot that gave him a buzz, sharpened his perceptions, speeded his reactions. He had spoken about it to Judith once. She had listened in silence. He could remem-ber the light coming in from the window in her old flat on the ridge above Lavender Hill, the summer haze that had hung over the valley of the Thames, the taste of her body and her sweat. She had drawn the sheet up to cover herself and turned away from him. He had put a hand on her shoul-der to turn her towards him again but she had resisted. 'What's wrong?' he'd asked. There'd been a silence. Then at last she had spoken. 'I don't like it when you talk like that. I can't explain. It makes me feel used. Something to give you a buzz. Was it always the same with you? If I were you I'd talk to your Wise Woman about it. I really would.'

Naturally he had talked about it, but as often happened in those sessions the talk had strayed uncontrollably to other matters. Why, for instance, he kept falling in love – which might not be unconnected with his search for adventure, for the thrill of the unknown, of sexual danger. Was that perhaps, the Wise Woman suggested, why he had been strangely reluctant to admit that he and Judith had got together? And had he wondered why? Was it wilful misunderstanding that made him answer defensively? Because they made a great team, he countered. In every possible way. At work, in bed and out of bed. Was that all? Well, he could see that she got work, make sure that she got compensation from the insurance company, which had been slow in coming up with the money after Kev's death till he got the union's lawyers on to them. Generally look after her. So he felt good, the Wise Woman commented. But had he ever considered that giving – emotional giving, which was what he seemed to be describing – can be an expression not of disinterested generosity but a way of dispensing bounty, like a lord of the manor handing out gifts that were a burden to the recipient and had sooner or later to be paid for; one that could in the long run become intolerable?

But he had been in no mood for caution. He was too drawn to this woman who stood apart from others he had known, in a sense an orphan of a war that was a legend in the history of the Left. He had genuinely been in love with her. As for Judith, she had certainly been dependent on him and, although she had never said so in quite those words, perhaps also 'in love'; but now he was aware that he was testing her love or whatever you cared to call it – their relationship – to destruction. Once they were safely back, they would have to talk it through. Maybe he would go back to the Wise Woman and try to work things out. He wasn't sure what the comrades would think if they discovered that he went to a shrink. He doubted if there would be more than the odd joke. And Comrade Siobhan, who would take him aside given half a chance and lecture him on bourgeois idealism, who was she to talk with that Indian homoeopath of hers, who had a bevy of young actresses totally dependent on him, getting them to strip off for a 'holistic' examination, feeding them little sugar pills, ordering them to go on retreats at his clinic somewhere in the Surrey hills. He found himself remembering how they had gone out selling the paper together and then found their way back to that posh house of hers off Ladbroke Grove, where the black boys roamed the streets and the police cars prowled to snap them up. 'You must get in among them, comrades,' said Comrade Fred, 'and recruit. We need the black youth. Go and get them.' But what Fergus chiefly recalled now was Comrade Siobhan's pink body and the fine reddish-gold colour of the hair on her skin.

He took a bend badly and almost ran out of road. As the car lurched, Judith was thrown against the door and wakened. 'Madrid,' he said, and indicated the light on the horizon. She made no reply but drew her coat tighter round her and settled back in the seat. 'Remember,' he said, 'if we're stopped you don't know any Spanish.' Stopped they were, flagged down by a couple of Guardia Civil and someone in plain clothes to whom the police handed the passports. One of the Guardia gave a cursory look into the back seat as the man returned their documents and, stepping back, waved the car on.

Fergus had felt the tingling sensation, the sudden outbreak of sweat at the base of the spine which he had first experienced as he waited outside the Rector's study to be caned for some breach of ridiculous rules; it was a sensation that had accompanied him into his adult life in moments of tension and danger. As they drove away he knew he must restrain the temptation to accelerate out of danger, to betray some sign of fear or uncertainty. It was not until they had reached a petrol station on the first outskirts of the city that he was able to relax, rubbing his hands on his trousers to remove the sweat. Then, while Judith paid the attendant, he extricated the paper with the address from under the mat beneath his feet and began to consult his town map.

The map we studied to find University City, the Manzañares, Puerta del Sol, Carabanchel: names we learned when the rebel armies were at the gates of the city; when the fate of Madrid and the Spanish Republic obsessed the hopes and fears of the Left; when we felt as if our own fates hung on the outcome of the battle; when our idealism was mobilized and in bleak housing estates the women were generous with pennies to buy milk for Spanish children; when a fellow-student was reported missing in the University City manning a machine-gun alongside German anti-fascists in the Thaelmann Battalion of the International Brigade; when truth and legend and lies were spun together by cynical propagandists; when the outcome was a defeat and a prologue to our own war that would be for many of us – but not for our rulers – an anti-fascist one.

The address, he saw, was in the northern suburbs – what looked like a new development near an industrial zone where, when they reached it, the blocks of flats rose separated by sandy terrain. The asphalt approach roads were deserted. As they drove slowly round Judith scanned the streets with names like Tetuan, Melilla, Ceuta – names celebrating the towns of Morocco where the dying man had made his reputation with the Foreign Legion; in July 1936 his rebel generals had seized power and the Civil War had started.

'Here,' she said at last and Fergus drew up before one of the blocks. There was no one about. The light from the street-lamps touched but did not illuminate the row of buttons by the door. But the name was clear enough: Menendez. A voice challenged them over the answer-phone, crackly, suspicious. '*Un amigo de Carlos,*' said Judith. She had her leather hold-all slung over her shoulder. She looked pale and tired. Fergus took her hand in what was intended as a gesture of thanks and reassurance; but though she did not withdraw it, neither did she return the pressure of his fingers.

The young man who opened to them came down quickly and noiselessly. In his twenties, bearded, he looked them up and down then, signalling them to follow quietly, led on up the stairs. On the top floor he left them for a few minutes in a little entrance hall; on the walls were a couple of cheap reproductions of dark-haired, doe-eyed children, half-smiling half-crying, a large handpainted plate that said *Recuerdo de las Canarias*, a poster for a *corrida*. Behind the door to their left there was a low hurried conversation. The young man emerged. *'Los chismos?'* he said. Fergus looked at Judith, who said it was in the car. The young man signed to Fergus to follow him outside. They were quickly back with the luggage. Then they disappeared again. Judith stood alone, heard the car start up and drive away.

The woman who at last came out to her was in her fifties. Greyhaired, small and round, squat, with a face that was oddly blunted – a mask that seemed to say its owner had experienced too much and had long since determined to let no feeling show. Without a word she turned and led Judith into a bedroom. It was almost like a young girl's. In one corner a floppy Harlequin doll shared a chair with a large pink teddy. On the bedside table there were knick-knacks – shells, glass figures – and a couple of photographs in silver frames – a young woman with a child, a handsome, middle-aged man. The dressing table was crowded with equipment laid out like tools or a surgeon's instruments: a silver-backed monogrammed mirror, nail scissors, a buffing pad, a tortoise-shell comb, a powder puff in a crystal bowl, scent bottles with sprays. Above the bed a crucifix and an image of the Sacred Heart with a sprig of dry palm leaf tucked behind it. On the wall at the bottom of the bed hung a huge framed photograph of a man in his forties, moustached, uncomfortable in collar and tie, dazed by the bright light of the studio. As Judith's glance lingered on it, the woman said: '*Mi padre.*' When Judith replied in Spanish the woman's face brightened. Was the man her husband, she wanted to know, her *novio*? Was she a comrade? No, said Judith, she wasn't. '*Pobrecita,*' said the woman.

Judith could think of various reasons why she might be considered a 'poor thing'. Which one did the woman have in mind, she wondered. In the small kitchen the woman cooked an omelette. She spoke little. But Judith had no appetite for food or talk. She looked at her watch. It was late. She would go to bed. She had a sudden feeling of being totally lost. Perhaps that was what the woman had guessed at, had read from her face – her sense of being abandoned. She slept soon and long.

They drove at a steady pace, but not so quickly as to attract attention, through the industrial zone, past warehouses and factories. Once or twice Fergus fancied he saw slogans painted on an expanse of wall. The road widened and then broadened out into a great avenue built for military parades and displays of power. Elaborate fountains gleamed in the dark. There had been no conversation; the driver's attention was on the road and the side-streets where once or twice Fergus thought he saw police vans parked in the shadows. But the street where they drew up was quietly residential. The driver signed to Fergus to take the suitcase, then led the way to a doorway where a quick word on the entry-phone admitted them to a ground-floor flat. There were two men in a room with dark furniture, a long dark table, dark high-backed chairs, a dark china cabinet on which stood a clock set on a black marble base and flanked by chastely naked girls. On the walls a couple of paintings of women in mantillas and men in black sombreros. Two men: one in his sixties with a long nose and balding hair.

Dressed in a dark suit with a pale tie he might have been a company lawyer or accountant but his face had the sallow tint Fergus had seen before on the faces of men who had passed long years in prison. The other, dark-haired, had the colouring you might see sometimes on the west coasts of Scotland or Ireland. Probably in his twenties, big and powerful, like a boxer or bouncer at a night-club. He could catch only an occasional word from their swift, low-voiced exchanges as they stood and talked, glancing from time to time in his direction. After a few minutes the driver shook hands with his comrades and left without a look or word for Fergus. The suitcase lay unopened on the table. From the street came the noise of the car starting up and driving away.

'Comrades, can I know what is going on?' Fergus asked with some patience. The two men disregarded the interruption. When he repeated it the young man turned to him with a *'Como? Como?'* But the older man held up a hand in a conciliatory gesture and to Fergus's surprise said in accented but reasonable English 'We will talk soon,' and continued his conversation. At last they fell silent. The young man, whom the Don called Luis (which might or might not have been his real name), drew the suitcase to him and began to unpack the contents and lay them out on the table. Explosives – which were no surprise to Fergus, who watched as the man, having fetched wire and tools from some inner room, began to work with quick fingers to assemble the bomb. The older man looked on in silence.

Suddenly, with a slight smile, he asked whether the comrade from London had ever read the story of the famous hidalgo Don Quijote de la Mancha. Fergus shook his head. But he knew the story, of course.

'The comrades here tell me I look like him. What a pity you don't know the original. It says he was *un hidalgo con los cincuenta años – de complexión recia, seco de carnes, enjuto de rostro.'*

The young man looked up from snipping at a length of wire and laughed.

'I will try to translate,' said the man. 'A gentleman of fifty years, with a – what do you say in English – tough complexion...'

'Coarse,' Fergus suggested. He had been involved in such puzzling and often dangerous games before, elaborate strategies – mazes of words through which one had to find one's way to get to the heart of the matter – strategies which were twin to his own rambling approaches to painful topics in the deceptive safety of the Wise Woman's room in Hampstead.

'Coarse – very good. *Seco de carnes*. Thin – no! – more than thin...'

'Skinny,' Fergus prompted.

'Skinny?'

'All skin and bone, my mother used to say.'

The comrade laughed. 'That is very good – skinny – all skin and bone. *Enjuto de rostro* – dried – like an old apple.'

'Wizened?'

'That is a new word, a good one – wizened in the face.'

It was a pleasure to talk to a comrade who understood the subtlety of language. Well, the description suited him because he too was pushing fifty, had a tough complexion and a skinny body. So Don Quijote was his *nom-de-guerre*. The comrade from London could call him that if he liked.

But now he must come to the point. And so he did. There was, he explained, a slight problem. It concerned the comrade's companion. Could he confirm that she was a comrade? No, said Fergus, but he was – wasn't that enough? The man shook his head. It might be all right in London where political activity meant selling papers, going on a picket line, but this was Madrid under a dictatorship. The comrade would no doubt know about the executions in September which had brought a hundred thousand workers out on strike. Then in October, a week after the dictator

83

had his heart attack, there had been ninety-six arrests. Since the beginning of November another ninety comrades had been rounded up in Malaga and Granada. No doubt there would be more firing squads, more garrotings, even if Franco was no more now than a living corpse. There were others who would see to it that his policy of repression continued. The ruling class did not surrender power just because the man to whom they had ceded power died. So it was a critical situation into which the comrade had brought a woman – his precise relationship to her was immaterial – who was not a member of the movement and therefore a potential security risk.

Fergus objected that Judith's father had died at the battle of the Jarama, in the International Brigade, but was aware as he spoke that it was an argument that would carry little weight. The man considered it for a minute then commented that there was no room in the struggle for sentimentality. Her father's death was neither here nor there. A lot of people had died in that war – not all of them Stalinists, like most of the International Brigade who had supported the rotten counter-revolutionary policies of the Third International and the Communist Party. The comrade must understand that.

Fergus recognized in the man's level tone, in his lack of rhetorical flourishes, a type of discourse he had encountered elsewhere, in South American republics, in South-East Asia, in the Lebanon, from the lips of men who had been so long in prison, in hiding, in underground struggles, that they considered without emotion their own life and death – as they did the life and death of others. He felt incongruously a threat that came not from the dictatorship and its agents but from men who were his own comrades in the struggle. He had accomplished his mission, he objected, had carried out the task set him by the comrades of the Central Committee in London. Indeed he had gone beyond his instructions in agreeing to take the suitcase and bring it to Madrid. The comrade must recognize that and allow him to get back to London – with his companion – and report on his mission.

The man Fergus now thought of as the Don listened carefully, nodding not so much in agreement, Fergus suspected, as to indicate that he had heard and understood what the other was saying. Yes, said the Don, but until the comrades in Madrid had come to a decision, the woman would be detained. She was being looked after by a woman who was not a comrade either. But they knew her. She had lost a son in the struggle. Shot in September along with other comrades. They could trust her. Meantime Fergus must wait. He would advise him to try to get some sleep.

Which was something Fergus prided himself on being able to do in almost any circumstances. It was a knack he had learned in his journeying to and fro across oceans and continents. In planes, trains and buses. In the back of cars. On floors in strange rooms where the mattress smelt of urine and the walls were marked by squashed bugs. In huts and luxury hotels. In the open under the bright incredibly near stars of the Cordilleras. In the chill of desert nights and the sticky heat of the jungle. Alone or with another. Sleep and food – without those it was not possible to function properly. Judith had sometimes reproached him for the way in which even at moments of difficulty in their relationship, times of tension when she had doubts about her role, about the nature of their attachment, pangs of jealousy over Siobhan – he had not only slept but had eaten with a healthy appetite. She experienced it as a kind of disregard, a certain coarseness of spirit. Tonight he had had no opportunity to eat, had in fact not eaten since the day before; but in the room where he had been told he would sleep there was at least a proper bed with a high, dark mahogany headboard. When the door closed he lay down fully dressed, pulled the cover over himself and, drawing his legs up like a child, slept.

When Judith woke it was day. There was no sign of Fergus. No voices through the wall. Only the sound of children playing in the sandy, windy spaces between the blocks and far away the whistle of a train, an occasional car driving past, the noise of an aircraft coming in low to land. She found the woman sitting in the kitchen. She was looking at an illustrated magazine with pictures of eminent persons coming and going to pay their respects to the great invalid. The woman had no news. No, she did not know when the men would be back. Meantime Judith must not go out. Must not go to the door, must not show herself at the windows. Judith drank a coffee. The woman said: 'I am Pilar.'

To pass the time they talked. About families. Pilar had a daughter and a son. There was no mention of a husband and Judith did not enquire. She had two granddaughters. One worked in a hotel. A good girl but she had a birthmark. The peasants said it meant her mother had had a desire for wine when she was pregnant. But that was superstition. And the other? A Carmelite nun. From a cupboard Pilar produced a box of photographs. Photographs of the man whose formal portrait had confronted Judith when she woke. As a young man. With his bride, who looked astonishingly young. Killed, said Pilar, in the defence of Madrid against the Fascists – in 1936 – in the very first days. Pictures of a girl dressed for her first communion. Pilar. Of a young woman wearing a silk blouse and a hat with a feather. Pilar again, in her twenties. Tarty, thought Judith and metaphorically bit her lip. 'Yes,' said the woman, 'that was me.' A goodlooking man in his forties, the father of Pilar's children. Pilar in a bathing costume, posing on a rock, leaning slightly forward towards the camera as if offering to whoever took the picture the promise of her breasts. Pilar in the snow in some mountain resort. Pilar with a group of women friends all dressed in the same way, at once conventional and coquettish. *Las chicas*, said Pilar, but gave no further explanation. Photographs of children decked out for their first communion. A girl and a boy, white and black, with gleaming patent leather shoes and in their gloved hands a breviary and a rosary.

Perhaps it was the photographs that formed the link, a sense of a shared destiny, of being exposed as women, fragile and yet, when the test came, strong, able to endure and to survive desertion, loss of love, the sense of being abandoned in a hostile world where men held power and sway over the minds and bodies of women. As the day wore on, Judith began to talk. Sometimes in a silence that fell between them or when Pilar was busy with some chore Judith reflected that she had not spoken so openly since she sat with her therapist who, courteous though he was and however content to let her spill out her fears, her puzzlements, her rage, had in some fundamental way failed to understand her pain and her need to fix an identity – even though it should be only through the gold symbol that hung round her neck.

So in the ambiguous safety of this room which was also her prison, she found herself speaking – as she had not spoken in his magician's cave – of what it was that drew her to Spain and to Madrid, of her desire to see Albacete and the Jarama. Pilar was a good listener, who intervened little and then with questions that were to the point. Some of them – they referred to her father's politics – Judith found it difficult to answer. Those about her time in Rome were easier and Pilar was clearly intrigued to learn about the colony of Spanish exiles, how they had earned their living, what Rome was like. She was unsurprised by the story of Sebastian's desertion on which her only comment was a grunt and a grimace.

It was when she came to talk of Kev that Judith, to her surprise, had the greatest difficulty, in the sense that she was overcome by sadness. It was not that she did not know that the sadness was still there; it was something she had carried about ever since the day of his death. But she had never before allowed it such expression. She was suddenly guiltily aware that in some way she had never properly mourned him – perhaps because, instead of allowing herself to experience his loss, she had taken refuge in her relationship with Fergus. Now as she spoke of his death on the icefields at the foot of the Eiger she was overcome by grief and wept, unashamedly wept, so that Pilar came to where she sat and held her. *Pobrecita*, she said, *pobrecita!*

It was not till the evening that – prompted by a question from Pilar – Judith at last came to speak about Fergus. Of how he had been good to her when Kev died but that now there were difficulties. Such as? Such as his political work, the way the Party took over his life and naturally – in a ridiculous way – hers too. Apart from everything else there was always the chance that he would be blacked for his politics; it had happened to others so why not to him? Then she would be the sole wage-earner and would have to take whatever work came her way, not strike out as a director. She was unsure how much Pilar understood of all that. Nor was she able to cast much light on his political work, which she herself found incomprehensible, remote and somehow inhuman. 'They speak about putting the world to rights, about justice and suffering; they say they have a kind of love for their fellow-men and women, but it's all terribly abstract. I could do with a little more love myself,' she said and was silent. Pilar watched reflectively for a little then said: 'I understand.'

For the rest of the evening they watched television, which was elegiac, solemn, hushed. The announcers were like undertakers' assistants, speaking quietly, lending to the details of the medical communiqués an almost religious tone, a mystical quality. They watched till the transmission closed with a salute to 'those who have fallen for God and Spain'.

Judith sat in front of the dressing-table and studied her

face in the mirror, identifying the traits she imagined she had inherited from her father, such as the prominent nose, the dark line of the eyebrows, the thick hair in which she had suddenly – just before they left London – discovered some grey and had asked herself how she would deal with it: let it turn grey naturally or dye it, henna it, buy some of the magic unguents they advertised on television? Why, she wondered, had she not talked about Itzak, born in Italy, son of Polish parents, twenty years old, whom she had met in the long vac in her second year at university?

His memory was bound up with tastes and perfumes of fruit – of grapefruit eaten straight from the tree, in slivers like a huge orange, of the melons they gathered in the fields of the kibbutz, of mint tea. She had lost her virginity in her first year in the back of a car in Regent's Park just beside the Zoo. Someone had flashed a torch at them as they struggled to put their clothes to rights. She had not been tempted to try again. But with Itzak she had gone swimming under the sandy cliffs at Kaiserya and for the first time felt with deep pleasure the warmth of the Mediterranean. Their love-making was saline, warm, full of strange and exciting new tastes. She thought: This is where I belong. She worked alongside him in the sun and made him teach her bits of Hebrew. He laughed and said: 'Why bother? We both speak English. You can teach me to speak better.'

When the season was over she lingered on and hitchhiked with him up to the Druse villages, where she bought the talismanic brass hand that was fastened to her bedroom door in London. There was much she did not understand, like the looks the Arab women gave as they passed them in the fields or in their villages high up on the hillsides. The anger of the young men who surrounded her taxi – the driver was an Arab – and pounded on the doors and windows because it was the Sabbath. The reactions of Itzak's parents when he took her home to meet them in their plain, sparsely furnished house on the outskirts of Tel Aviv. His father was a building worker; his mother was large, square, dark, voluble, constantly washing, constantly cooking. She spoke to Itzak not in Hebrew but in Polish or Yiddish. She did not address Judith directly.

On Judith's second or third visit, she pointed at Judith's Star of David and made some remark to Itzak.

'What did she say?' Judith asked afterwards.

'Oh, nothing important really. She just wondered why you wear it. Wondered if you knew what it means to wear that star.'

'It means,' Judith replied, 'that my father was a Jew. Did you tell her?'

Itzak nodded.

'She asked was your mother a Jew. She just thinks you're lucky. None of your people went to the camps.'

'Did you tell her he died fighting Fascism?'

Itzak nodded.

'She said if he wanted to die fighting he should have come and fought as a Jew for a Jewish homeland.'

The vacation was running out. She had almost come to the end of her money. They had found a place – a friend's room – where they would spend the night and talk. She was going to come back next year, she said. Would he wait for her? 'Judith,' he said, 'you don't understand. Your mother wasn't Jewish, so neither are you. You're what my mother calls a *schikse*. I could never have you as a permanent girl-friend.' She had got up and put on her things. 'It's not that I don't like you,' he added sadly, apologetically. 'That we don't have a good time together. But I can't – I have to be honest with you.'

She got a plane back to London after two miserable days. She had not told Fergus about it. Had never mentioned it to her mother. Could not find the courage to talk about it even to a stranger like Pilar. But she had talked to her therapist who had been patient, reasonable, calm, as he always was, talking about cultural and religious differences, reminding her that Itzak was right. Her mother was not Jewish so she could not be Jewish either. She must try to understand Itzak. 'But he was prepared to fuck me,' she said. The man nodded. There was obviously a power situation there and he could understand that she felt that Itzak had taken advantage of it. But had she thought about Itzak's position? Did she think he had loved her? Yes? Then perhaps his predicament had been as painful as hers. She sat in silence for what seemed an interminable time till the man dismissed her. As she left and walked out into the leafy Hampstead avenue, she knew she would never again return to his quiet room with the cacti, its vaguely abstract prints and on the desk a collection of pebbles, worn smooth, which he would sometimes handle as a metaphor for the shaping power of memory. She had not forgotten Itzak and his betrayal. Her anger at it was as lasting as her resentment of her dead father, the deserter who even from the dead had the power to mark her as different.

In the anteroom of death the muted exchanges continued. The question repeated to each newcomer, repeated in corners, received with a nod of the head or a raising of the eyebrows was: Have you seen the *Nuevo Diario*? The editorial that says 'the Leader's life depends on some wires, some machines, some artificial power and, of course, Providence. Good God, enough!'? There were those who shook their heads and wondered what would happen if in the course of time the process of liberalization, of 'democratization', went much further. They had gloomy forebodings which they expressed to each other in little huddles. Only the bravest or rashest or most honest allowed themselves to raise an eyebrow at the parenthetical mention of Providence. But such cynicism was far from the mind of the girl from Los Huertos who sat by a small table not far from the bedside where a shaded light allowed her to see the text she had brought with her to pass the hours of vigil: *The Road of Perfection* by Santa Teresa of Avila, whose life and work had been commemorated in the convent just two days before the dying man had his heart attack and therefore three days before the young nun was summoned by the Mother Superior to be told that she had been chosen to assume the responsibility of attending the great man in his last moments. When she heard that she had been called, she went into the chapel to pray, remembering the souls of the dead and the dying, remembering her grandmother who had sinned so greatly but who would surely be forgiven if she had in her old age repented her life, and remembering her sister exposed to such moral dangers in the hotel where she worked.

A dark-suited doctor came in and inclined his head to the crucifix above the death bed. Then he busied himself, feeling a pulse, scanning the waveform on the oscillograph screen, checking the wires that transmitted the irregular, faltering but unceasing rhythm of the heart beat. Then he backed away from the bed, came over to the nun and asked in a low, controlled whisper: 'Any change?' The nun, who had risen at his entrance, shook her head. The man made a gesture with his hands as if to say 'Patience' then turned and slipped out of the room.

Fergus wakened to find the door of his room locked. He had an urgent need to piss and knocked on the door but no one came. Prising open the window he contrived to let his urine splash down into the courtyard. He knocked again and then banged and shouted. Steps came running and the door was brusquely opened by Luis, the young man with the dark hair, excited and angry. Fergus sat himself down at the table where he had been questioned the night before. On it lay a handgun, cleaning gear and a cardboard box of bullets. The young man sat down and went on cleaning the weapon. '*Comer,*' said Fergus and signalled his hunger. The man shrugged. So they sat and watched each other.

Fergus thought of the irony of it all. Here were two comrades engaged in the same struggle, yet what lay between them was the threat of the gun. It was a relief therefore when there was a ring at the door bell and after a short parley Don Quijote appeared, carrying a shopping bag containing some tapas, bread and smoked ham, a bottle of wine.

'How long is this to go on for?' Fergus asked as the food was laid out on a plate. The Don shrugged. 'As long as necessary. So eat!' Fergus ate. When they were finished the Don said he was sorry but Fergus had to go back into the bedroom. Fergus protested, which caused the young man to say something and laugh. The older man nodded: 'Comrade,' he said, 'it is better you go.' Was there no way he could get in touch with his companion, let her know that he was safe? Fergus asked as he moved towards the bedroom door. The Don considered. 'Perhaps,' he said. 'Someone will tell her. I promise. But now – bedroom.'

Reluctantly Fergus found himself sitting on the bed and heard the key turn in the lock. He went to the window and peered out through the gap he had opened but he could see only a patch of wall some twenty feet away. He pulled at the slats of the persiennes but he could make out little except that the window – as he had guessed – gave on to a courtyard surrounded on all sides by stone walls. In the room itself there was little furniture: an old-fashioned dressing-table with a ewer and basin. In one corner a small black crucifix, under it a kind of prie-dieu with a cushion worn by pious knees. Whose house was this, he wondered, that the comrades had been able to commandeer; the house of some respectable middle-class man or woman, some widower or widow, the grandmother or aunt (recently dead) of some comrade who could without raising suspicion choose it as an operational base in this respectable neighbourhood? He had to take his hat off to them.

His examination of the furniture, of the chest with its empty drawers still smelling of lavender, was interrupted by the sound of voices in the room beyond. They continued for a couple of hours. A meeting, he concluded. As he listened, he believed he could distinguish the voice of the Don, dominant but calm, even, cutting through argument and debate. Was he, he wondered, the subject of their discussion? Would he be given the chance to dispel the doubts and distrust they had expressed on his arrival in the house (which was something Fergus could forgive them)? There was a tradition and a need – especially in conditions of illegality – for comrades to be security conscious. He remembered Comrade Fred at their first meeting producing the listening device. Since then he had become familiar with the precautions at the Boatyard: the guards at the main gate at night who – given the danger of an attack by Fascists and skinheads – were armed with wooden pick-helves; which was something the comrades knew they must not speak about. Naturally he had been unable to tell Judith, to warn her adequately about the security measures at the gates. She had been left to encounter their rigour one evening when she came to pick him up – they were going out to an Indian meal – and had trouble when she rang the bell, which sounded far away behind the high perimeter wall. At last someone had come and opened the gate a few inches while still keeping it on the chain. Then she had been interrogated about who she was and why she wanted to speak to a comrade.

So the evening had begun badly and ended worse, with accusations on her part of paranoia and ridiculous games; on his, with exasperation at her failure (or refusal) to understand how exposed the Party was – a target for attempts at penetration by the security services, for provocations, for physical attacks. She had shrugged and said she hoped that some day he might have the guts to break out of the fantasy world in which he increasingly lived. She was getting fed up to the teeth with these interminable meetings that were called at ridiculously short notice and went on half the night – which was either incompetence or a kind of bullying – like the weekend summer schools and the rallies where he turned up like a good boy and where no doubt he enjoyed the company of Siobhan. She was not sure she could cope with it much more. It was up to him.

The mention of Siobhan was an error which she recognized too late and which he seized on. It allowed him to protest that just because he – as she would no doubt put it – 'fucked' Siobhan, not very often and in any case a good long time ago, this did not mean that there was some passionate thing going on with her. He knew that the memory of that evening still rankled with her, that her distaste for the comrades had not grown any less; but at least she had come with him on this trip even if it might well be their last one together. When they got back to London they would discuss things soberly like two adults and see where they went from here. What couldn't go on was cohabitation, this co-existence as a couple round whom estrangement had built its icy ramparts.

The key turned in the lock. It was the Don, as Fergus now called him in his mind. With a smile he apologized for locking him up but the comrade would understand the need for security. They sat at the table which was littered with the signs of the long meeting – full ashtrays, empty glasses and coffee cups, an almost empty bottle of *fino*. Would Fergus like a drink? asked the Don, and handed a couple of glasses to Luis who went off, reluctantly, to clean them.

Over the *fino*, the talk began. What he was interested in, said the Don, was the kind of job Fergus did. He was, he said, very ignorant about such matters. Where to begin, thought Fergus, how to describe the process of documentary film-making, the hierarchies of the institutions, the editorial choices, the codes that were permitted and those not in terms of the words and images one could use, the nature of montage and the cunning that allowed a subversive reading to be inserted in a film. The Don listened with apparent attention. Then he switched to another tack. Could the comrade tell him something about the work of the Party in London, in England? Tell him a little about this famous Boatyard? What was a 'boatyard' really? Fergus said nothing for a little, then he replied: 'I do not know you. You may be a comrade but I cannot discuss matters with you that might be a breach of Party security.' The Don considered his answer. 'Very interesting,' he said, whether with approval or disapproval Fergus did not know. 'But it is time to go back into the room.'

As he sat on his bed Fergus knew he could do nothing but let time pass. This too was an experience he was used to, hours of waiting for a telephone to ring or a contact to materialize. What was important was not to fret at the slowness of time's passing but to surrender to it. Refusal to surrender could mean falling into a state of impatience and frustration which was exhausting, unproductive, liable to lead to errors of judgement, rash decisions – in extreme cases to hysteria and a kind of madness. It was a lesson, he had told his Wise Woman, that he had learned from a man who had spent fifteen years on Robben Island with Mandela. She nodded in agreement and suggested that it was something he ought to think about more. This he had done and in due course had brought her like a proud schoolboy the thought that we were all serving a sentence of unknown duration which might stretch out for years and decades or end tomorrow. The only way to cope with the discovery was to take time as it came, without impatience, letting it run through us like a current that could neither be slowed nor hastened. In that way – he uttered the words with some embarrassment – we might make a good end. She had said:

'I think "good ends" are important. With age you will find they become more so.'

So he allowed himself to relax on the bed and watched a fly circle the lampshade and explore the ceiling. From time to time he dozed a little, disturbed, brought back to himself by the sound of the street door, of voices that rose and then died away. Once when the noise woke him from a leaden bout of sleep he took back into consciousness the memory of a dream of which he could recollect clearly only that his mother had been there with her trug and secateurs drifting, in that curious way she had, through some sort of park.

He resolved that when he was back in London he would go oftener to the home where she sat, remote from the world, in the fog of Alzheimer's – not just when he felt guilty after a gap of months which he would explain away to the nurses and the matron as due to the nature of his job, the travel, the long spells abroad. They had proof of the truth of his excuses in the postcards he sent her from Rio, Caracas, Bangkok, Seoul, and which they arranged on a kind of noticeboard in the room where the old woman (not so old, really; only seventy-four) existed uncomprehendingly. Sitting by the chair where she sat with a blanket over her knees, he would wonder what memories glimmered behind her eyes to make them light up sometimes and bring a smile to her face.

It was her smile that moved and troubled him as much as anything else, for it was with just such a smile that she had confronted life: the rudeness of her husband, the disdain of Sarah for her social timidity, her shyness when she had encountered Judith's mother and had sipped like a girl at a gin and tonic and listened to denunciations of men, of politics, of the ingratitude of children. It was the smile with which – when he was eleven or twelve – she had cuddled him, drawing him to her breast with a rare gesture of affection, after his father had raged at him for not being sufficiently manly, for being frightened of the hard ball that hurtled towards him at the practice nets. If he drew himself away from her embrace it was because her softness, the scent that rose from her warm skin, obscurely disturbed him. As he did so her smile faded and turned to sadness just as it did when she said goodbye on the platform at the end of the hols, or of his embarkation leave in 1945 and the train took him off on a journey that ended in the anti-climax of peace.

The truth was that he could hardly bear to see her and his visits were more for the benefit of the staff (who got boxes of chocolates at Christmas when he remembered) and the matron (fortyish, plump, widowed with two children) who was a faithful viewer of his programmes. Once (being deeply depressed) he had got tight and narrowly escaped ending up in her bed.

The moment he got back to London he would drive down to the coast and submit to the pain of a visit. At least the fog of forgetting had hidden from her (or so he imagined) the sight of her husband declining into alcoholism and ridiculous dotage before dying of a stroke on a boozy trip from Newhaven with a boatload of cronies, members of a breakfast club bound for a day of wine and oysters in Dieppe. The whole business of getting the body back, of dealing with the French authorities, with the British consul had been complicated and time-consuming. Fergus had discharged his filial duties but without sorrow, without any real sense of mourning – only a residual sense of being unprotected, as if the death of a parent had exposed him to the inevitability of his own end which might come, not in some more or less heroic or exciting circumstance but sordidly, in a hospital with tubes and wires and drips, until his heart or his lungs packed up. He imagined Judith coming to see him in his last days and her sorrow at his passing. But he recognized as he turned over and tried to sleep once more that this was merely a maudlin self-pitying fantasy.

They were sitting in the bleak dining-room with its forbidding furniture. Fergus had breakfasted on coffee and a roll. There were two others there apart from the Don. One was the youngish man from the night before; the other was slim with a narrow face and quick, darting dark eyes. Fergus had seen people like him in Central America, where such features were the legacy of the Aztecs. Beyond that he was able – though he understood only the occasional word – to identify the man's accent as South American without the lisp of Castilian. He was aware that the man was referring to him, glancing in his direction, making a point by gesture, stabbing at the table with a finger and then leaning back in his chair as if he had completed his case.

'*Bueno*,' said the Don turning to Fergus. 'As I said last night, we have a problem about your companion. We understand she speaks excellent Spanish. We have also learned that she had a lover in Republican refugee circles in Rome. Now these circles were Stalinist. They were also penetrated by the Spanish security services. So the relationship with this woman is important and raises a number of questions. One is: how does it come that you as a member of the Fourth International have as your companion a woman with such dubious political relationships in her past? But it seems there is another difficulty.' Fergus was about to interrupt but the Don held up his hand in a peremptory gesture that silenced him.

'The second problem is this. The comrade here says that he knows of you from South America. That you were in Nicaragua and had contacts with the Contras. In fact that you visited a Contra headquarters and interviewed various people there. You do not speak Spanish so you had an interpreter. That man was known to the comrades in Nicaragua as a traitor, an informer and probably a CIA agent.' Fergus opened his mouth but the Don did not let him interject a word. 'Now we know – because there is a great deal of evidence from a number of countries – that people like yourself who work in television and who claim to be investigating, to be discovering the truth for the bourgeois media, have often close links with the intelligence agencies of the capitalist West. We know of cases in Venezuela, in Chile, in Nicaragua, the Lebanon. I could go on. You will no doubt realize, comrade – if you are a comrade – that this is a very serious situation. I have been instructed by our central committee to investigate and to take appropriate action.'

The man with the South American accent interrupted. The Don heard him out patiently, shook his head and turned again to Fergus: 'Comrade,' he said, 'you are going to have to convince us.'

Fergus sat in silence. He was running his finger round the rim of his plate, a gesture of which he became absurdly aware as he raised it to his mouth and sucked at the sweetness of the jam. The calm and even tone of this comrade-prosecutor caused a pang of fear which he now attempted to master by draining the last drops of coffee in his cup. He was, he realized, before what amounted to a people's court, which would not hesitate to pass sentence on him and carry it out. Some of the deaths he had seen in the course of his job had been not the result of rage and violence but of cool decisions taken as a matter of necessity, to protect the security of a party, a group, for the good of the cause. Because in certain circumstances a revolutionary cannot take risks. Because too much is at stake: the safety and lives of too many comrades, which outweigh the life of an individual convicted – or even suspected – of being a danger to the organization, or of betrayal.

That night Judith slept badly. A noise woke her. Voices. The sound of a door shutting. Then silence. She sat up in bed and was gripped by anxiety. She had not felt such deep indefinable fear since the night she heard that Kev was dead.

The room was dark. The geography unfamiliar. She recognized the tightness in her temples that presaged a migraine. She lay and felt it develop. At last nausea drove her to grope her way to the bathroom. In the little hallway no light seemed to come from under any door. She wondered where Pilar slept. Or had she been left alone with the flat door safely locked? She was miserably, noisily sick, retching into the lavatory basin. But no one came. At last she made her way back to her room. Her eyes now accustomed to the dark could make out the dressing-table, the mirror in which she moved a pale ghost. Black and white like the little roll of film hidden away at the back of her desk. A film editor had sent it to her, a friend of Kev's and a witness at their wedding. She had not had the courage to look at it but she knew what it showed. It was, after all, a famous shot that whirled into black and death. Suddenly, with immense fear, she felt that death was lying in wait in this flat where she was held prisoner. She lay down, drew the sheet over her head as she had used to do as a child and towards dawn at last fell asleep.

All next day she lay in the darkened room, rising from time to time to be sick. Once or twice Pilar came to see her. Sympathetic, attentive, supportive, she offered tea – *un tecito* – aspirins, enquired whether Judith by any chance was pregnant. She herself had suffered terribly from morning sickness. Then she left Judith to her pain and nausea, which she struggled to overcome by sleep. Pilar was stirring early next morning and Judith rose to join her. Pilar closed the shutters when Judith shielded her eyes against the light. 'Is there any news?' she asked but Pilar shook her head.

Off and on through the day Pilar talked in snatches that added up to a narrative interrupted by little tasks – sweeping the floor, washing some clothes, making coffee, drinking a *fino*, cooking some plain rice for Judith: a sure cure for bouts of sickness. By telephone calls – usually curt ones which Judith tried to decode but lacked sufficient clues. Longer ones with what were clearly with women friends.

Enquiries about their health, their children and grandchildren. Complaints about the price of food. Exchanges of information about other women friends. Gossip that occasionally made Pilar's face relax into a smile and then laughter as she sat with her legs splayed to show the network of broken veins on her inner thighs. *'Las chicas,'* she explained, 'we used to work together. At Chicote's. We still keep in touch.' Did she know about Chicote's? She would tell her later but now she had to shop. Again she warned Judith to keep away from the windows and not to answer the door or the telephone. Judith watched her go. Her legs were still those of a sturdy peasant girl but patterned with knotted veins. Her whole body was squat and compact, solid, graceless, blunted like her face. As she went out with her curious rolling gait she grumbled at the stairs and the fatigue of her errand. Judith wondered but could not imagine what she had been like when she worked with *las chicas*.

Late in the evening there was a call to which Pilar replied with little more than monosyllables: *'Sí! Sí! Ya. Está bueno.'* Judith knew from the studied way in which Pilar looked away that the call concerned her. So when Pilar laid down the receiver she asked directly. Pilar did not deny it. No, she said, there was no news and no one Judith could call. Her friend was safe. 'We must be patient,' she added, 'we are women and know how to be patient. That's what men expect of us.' Then she switched on the television for a moment before turning it off again dismissively. In bed that night Judith lay awake and to distract herself put together in her head the story of Pilar's life, which had not been told in these exact terms nor in an ordered way but disjointedly across the day. It had been a ploy on Pilar's part, an immense diversion to keep her thoughts off her plight and what lay in wait in the future. A kindness.

I was born in Madrid near the prison at Carabanchel. As a

child I used to see the women queuing with food for their men-folk. Gipsies mainly. But other women too. Their men were criminals, murderers, thieves. Political prisoners as well. My father always said that Carabanchel was a monument to class rule and the oppression of the workers. There were no señores in Carabanchel. Only ordinary people. He was a tram-driver. A union member. In the CGT. A member of the Communist Party. My mother was a peasant woman from Los Huertos. She came to Madrid as a servant. I don't know how my father met her but they got married. I think she was fifteen. She was pregnant with me.

I was twelve when the Civil War came. My father joined the militia when the Fascists attacked Madrid. He had done his military service and knew how to handle a rifle. He was killed in the first week of the siege. In the University City where Franco's Moorish troops were fighting from building to building and from floor to floor. We never learned where he was buried. I was there when the German planes came and bombed Madrid. My mother took me into the Metro and we listened to the explosions. One day we looked up and there was a fighter plane, a Russian one with red stars on its wings. On our side. The people in the streets shouted and cheered. That I can remember. And I remember the day – it was the 8th of November 1936 – when I saw the soldiers of the International Brigade march through the streets and straight to the front. It was a wonderful day. People said they saved Madrid.

When my father was killed my mother joined the militia too and went to the front. She was wounded – not badly. They sent us to Albacete, the base for the International Brigades, where she worked as a nurse in a hospital. By the time I was a woman the Civil War was over. We had lost. They came and arrested my mother and me. We ended up in Carabanchel. It was very bad. The cells were crowded. There was not much food and what there was was bad. Every night we were wakened by the firing-squads working in the courtyard. Then on 5th August 1939, when the war had been over almost four months, they came at night and took forty people – boys and girls, men and women – and shot them. They said it was some sort of reprisal but I never knew the truth. My mother was one of them. She was just thirty.

When I got out of jail I had nowhere to go. I went back to Los Huertos but no one wanted to know the daughter of a Red. So I went back to Madrid. I thought I might get a job as a maid. But I met a woman who had been in jail with my mother and me. She took me to a friend of hers with a flat off the Gran Via. Señora Concepcion. (Here Pilar laughed.) So I started to work in a place called Chicote's. It's still there, in the Gran Via. A bar and a lot of tables. The men would come in and order a drink at the bar. A fino. As they drank they would be looking round to see which of the *chicas* was there tonight, deciding who it was they fancied. Once they'd made up their minds they'd come over to her table and offer her a drink. They'd talk a little, about the last corrida and who was going to fight the bulls next week. All kinds of men. Businessmen, professors, students, journalists, actors, officers, members of the Falange. Not many workers. We were too expensive. If they weren't regulars – people from the provinces maybe – they'd discuss the price. Then we'd take them off to Señora Concepcion's flat. She took her cut. I'd be back in twenty minutes – half-an-hour at the most. So I made a living.

I had lover. He was called Manuel. A *torero*. Not one of the great ones. Like me he came from Los Huertos. When he was a kid he used to practise with other boys in the square in front of the church. They had these horns fixed on a long stick and he had his *muleta* and when one of his mates charged him he would hold it out and do a *veronica*. You know about a *veronica*? No? One of the most exciting passes a *torero* can do. We used to go often – *las chicas* – and have fun. Good seats – *sol y sombra* – half sun, half shade. Sometimes, if we liked a client, we'd let him take us and then maybe come back home afterwards. But I never liked it when Manuel was out there fighting the bulls – which wasn't very often. He never made it to the really big corridas here in Madrid, in Seville or Valencia. It was in the provinces he fought the bulls and over the Pyrenees in France. He chased women and death. I think he got the same kick out there in the ring when he felt the breath of the brave bull in his face as he did when he made love to me – or to any other whore. In the end he was not good in bed. Because he was getting frightened in the ring. A bull gored him in Albacete and he almost died in hospital.

After he got involved in *estraperlo*. Do you know what *estraperlo* means? You do? Right, so he was in the black market. These were the good days. We went to the Canarias. To the mountains in winter. He had plenty of money. He gave me a son and a daughter. Then he was put away for five years. I used to take him food in Carabanchel every week. There's a café just by the prison where we used to meet – all the women with men inside. Some under sentence of death. When he got out he went south to Malaga. He said he would send for me but he never did. He got into the construction business and made a mint of money. He found someone else but still used to send me some and then he stopped sending it. But I didn't want his money.

After that there were others but my true love was Manuel. I went on working till I had saved enough to buy a little shop in the suburb – selling fruit and vegetables – the usual things. Juanita runs it for me – she used to work in Chicote's. My daughter got herself pregnant and went back to Los Huertos. She had two daughters. I've told you about them already – the nun and the chambermaid. My son was active in one of the parties of the Left. The Red Flag or some such name. They called themselves Maoists. I told him they were mad. They blew up some policeman and he was arrested. They sentenced him to death and shot him.

As she listened, Judith had recalled images from the Civil War which she had collected as a teenager from magazines and papers and pasted in a scrapbook, in spite of her mother's exhortations to forget it, to leave history alone, that it never did anyone any good to go digging up the past. Among the pictures she remembered the face of a young girl (Pilar?) looking up in terror to the sky as the bombs fell from the black birds of the German Condor Legion which had miraculously been challenged by the stub-nosed Soviet fighters. Later, when she was a student, she had attended a weekend summer school on the documentary film as history. There she had seen images she could not get rid of. The defence of Madrid. Falling bombs. Barricades of paving stones and wood, bits of furniture. Militia men and women firing from behind them. A dead horse. A shot of men from the International Brigades which she wished she could run again and again in case among the faces she might see that of her father. Perhaps Pilar had been luckier and had caught his eye as he went to face his first battle – the one he survived, only to die six months later in the valley of the Jarama.

But if Judith could provide in her mind so many images to go with the first part of Pilar's story, she had few to accompany it beyond the final collapse of the Republic. And of that she had only those of refugees in the snow – men, women and children, and disbanded troops crossing the French frontier in the bitterness and despair of defeat. She took up from the bedside table the silver-mounted photographs of a woman in her late twenties perhaps, a broad face with strong dark eyebrows glancing down at the little girl in her arms. Judith could imagine her words of encouragement as she coaxed the child to look into the lens. Her features had not yet been blunted yet she must by this time have been working in Chicote's for several years. The young woman who had bought – or been given more likely – the floppy doll that was draped in the chair and before she set out to her work had used the powder puffs in their crystal bowls on face and bosom, had sprayed the scent and rubbed it on hands and neck. But beyond that ritual moment Judith could not accompany her, nor imagine how she had submitted to the commerce of sex with its tariff and rules. She had herself occasionally slept with a man on an impulse, responding to an invitation that was sometimes oblique, sometimes direct, that sometimes emanated from herself in response to a physical need, a desire to be held, to find a moment of closeness. Sometimes they had been pleasurable, these moments; sometimes the source of disappointment and a kind of revulsion from which she had recovered by a period of celibacy. She presumed that it was this experience extended over a working life-time – repeated how many times a day and for how many years? – that had shaped the mask Pilar now presented to the world.

It made Judith wonder about the men, the clients. It was something she had never discussed with Fergus, who was secretive about his past experiences. But he had travelled the world, had been places where girls were sold to entrepreneurs for an industry in which the workers mimed the experience of making love – performing the act more or less skilfully, no doubt. She would ask him. Ask him to explain, too, what men – what he – hoped to get out of their encounters. Whether she would get a straight answer was another matter.

Restlessly Judith turned on the light by her bed, rose and felt in her big leather bag for her notebook. She had entered only the occasional jotting since they came to Spain. To write in it she needed to be alone and there had been no chance of that in any of the hotels in Madrid and on their way to the rendezvous with the friend of Carlos. Inexpensive hotels except for a parador (a Disney-like castle) chosen because it lay just beyond a battle-field where Fergus had kicked up some scraps of iron, a bullet case and a crumpled piece of metal which he maintained was a cap badge. An oppressive place, with sombre furniture and sombre prints on the walls. It was off-season and they seemed to be the only guests. That night they had had a problem because she had not wanted to make love and Fergus had accused her of being cold, of being jealous for no reason, for being unspeakably prim and bourgeois. Maybe they ought to think seriously about their relationship, because he really didn't see how they could go on like this. All he wanted was a certain affection, a minimum of warmth – including sex now and again. No, he wasn't saying that he had rights over her and her body. But he certainly didn't go along with the feminists and that stuff about the politics being personal; that was a massive distraction from the real struggle which was genuinely political, based on the class struggle which in turn encompassed women's struggles. All the sisters did was to muddy the waters with absurd resolutions at annual conference which the Right-wing then voted for – completely cynically, of course – thus blocking important resolutions from the Left.

She had tried to sleep but he had sat up cleaning his finds, rinsing them under the taps in the handbasin and then brushing them to remove the impacted earth and mud. Next morning he was in a better mood, came and sat on her bed and kissed her on the cheek and then, like a child, displayed his treasures. It really was a cap-badge – but he couldn't say whether French or British – and a piece of horse-shoe and a fragment of a cannon-ball. And then something quite different, the cartridge case of a modern rifle bullet – French probably – from the Civil War. It was as if he had kicked up layers of history. He had been thinking, too. Maybe there should be a stills sequence from Goya's *Disasters of War* – he hadn't seen any reproductions for ages so couldn't be specific, but these were timeless images of cruelty – and what about Picasso's *Guernica*? Turning the pages of her notebook she found the entry she had made:

Goya: Los Desastros de la Guerra – publisher?
Picasso: Guernica – rights?

She had written it in the margin opposite an image sketched in words by that rifleman who was her chief guide through Goya's disasters:

There was a Frenchman burnt in the grass. Drawn up like a dried frog. The miserable fate of the poor fellow called forth from us very little sympathy but seemed only to be a subject of mirth.

It had reminded her of Sebastian sitting at a café-table in Rome with friends of his father – exiled veterans of the Civil War – and laughing (as if he had heard it for the first time) at the story of how some joker had propped a dead Moor, frozen stiff in the cold of the Sierra, up against a tree with one arm raised in a parody of the Fascist salute.

But what she sought now in her bedroom under the photograph of the man who had fought and died in the defence of Madrid was a clump of notes on women. There was the British officer taking a high moral tone and accusing the French of being accompanied by 'a host of undesirable females'. When she found the passage she had laughed over it with Fergus, who had wondered whether they included that young woman in hussar's uniform reported to be inseparable from the French commander Masséna, one of Napoleon's marshals. So much so that one morning, when his troops were already engaged in their attempt to storm the British positions, a despatch-rider had had to hammer on his bedroom to fetch him from her side. Judith had tried to imagine this young woman, who flashed through the smoke and confusion of war, dressing her in her mind in the fashion of those contemporary coloured prints where impossibly slim dandies displayed the fine feathers of death.

French hussar – light blue uniform – tight white breeches – a cloak on one shoulder – a tasseled pouch (sabretache?) hanging from the sword-belt – a cloak on one shoulder – on the head a Polish shako set at an angle.

Very sexy, her notes went on, *bisexual? a military groupie? a mascot? or a rebellious spirit – her own woman – defiant – with the courage to follow her desires – for sex – for excitement.*

Why should she be blamed because her lover lost that battle?

Masséna – Italian sailor and smuggler – commissioned in the revolutionary army – Maréchal de l'Empire – Duke of Rivoli. But what about his hussar? What evidence that she wasn't merely a fiction in the minds of the male historians and peddlers of anecdotes – a projection of desires and fantasies, an erotic stereotype? The distortions of the male gaze like a refracted image in water. An invention to set against the sober image of the British commander at that same battle. Alone, on the skyline on his horse as the French advanced uphill. Then a wave of his hat and a shouted command got the infantry on to its feet. Their rolling fire blasting the attacking French column. And the Marshal was still in bed with his hussar. Too good to be true!

Along with her blue hussar she had put the maid of Saragossa, whom Goya had shown holding the match to the touch-hole of a cannon, defiant, courageous. But not the sort of heroine the imagination of Judith's rifleman required:

'I saw the heroine of Saragossa the other day. A heroine of all the world ought to be beautiful. But nature has bestowed on her a visage so much in opposition to my idea of beauty that with all my previous determination I could not fall in love with her. She was dressed in a jacket turned up with red and had half-boots and pantaloons – a huge cutlass hung by her side.'

The sheer effrontery of the man, Judith now wrote, leaning forward to get the light on her notebook. *What would he have made of Pilar's mother at the barricades in the outskirts of Madrid?*

NB Look up the British press and see what they had to say about the women soldiers on the Republican side. Photos? Butch stereotypes?

Rereading her notes, Judith wondered how to describe her

own role. Wasn't she herself a mere camp-follower? Good for a cuddle and a bit of sex but someone who could be discarded, excluded from decision-making that affected her own life in a situation which she knew to be dangerous – excluded by men who were at bottom contemptuous of women – men like Comrade Fred with his handmaidens who would no doubt be rewarded when the great day came. She felt her anger grow within her, so that when she put out the light at last she had a restless and broken sleep.

In the palace where the dictator lay suspended between life and death, a group of men sat round a table in a small room. For the most part they were elderly, military men some of them, one with a bullet scar on his cheek; others (politicians these) were on the whole younger, dark-suited, some wearing dark glasses although it was already dark outside; one a priest – a prince of the church rather – with pectoral cross and episcopal ring which the more devout had bent to kiss as he extended his hand to them. Yet though he sat at the head of the table, he was not the chairman of the meeting; the Church deferred to politics in the person of the cabinet minister with his undertaker's face and the calm voice that spoke of power and the consciousness of power. They had come together, he explained, with the assent of and in the presence of His Excellency the Cardinal Archbishop to consider the Caudillo's message to the Spanish nation – that nation which he had served so faithfully as soldier, leader and head of state, who had led them to victory against communism, freemasonry and godlessness.

He himself would personally deliver the message to the Spanish nation on television and on radio. It would be carried by all the press and delivered from pulpits throughout the country. But before they began their sad duty of discussing the text, he called upon the Cardinal Archbishop to bless their deliberations; which the prelate duly did in sonorous Latin phrases, familiar but taking on new significance in the presence of death. *In nomine patris et filii et spiritus sancti* said the rich episcopal voice in conclusion and the bejewelled hand was raised in blessing.

There was a moment's silence before the minister, with a slight, dutiful inclination of his head to the prelate, loosened the tape securing a folder with dark leather covers and extracted from it a document which he laid on the table before him, running the back of his hand over it lightly as if to remove any slightest wrinkle.

It was a document, he explained, drawn up at a moment when the political situation in the nation was different from what obtained today. The text as it stood, he continued, stressed the Caudillo's wish to live and die a Catholic. He therefore asked for pardon for all his sins and for forgiveness for his enemies – by whom the minister believed the Caudillo meant those who tragically, mistakenly, had taken up arms against the Nationalist crusade. In a spirit of reconciliation, the text explained that the Caudillo had not considered them as such. This, in the speaker's humble opinion – but he would defer to the advice of His Excellency and to the consensus of the meeting if one could be achieved – was a point that ought to be reinforced in the new political climate and the precise form of words discovered that matched the state of the nation at this solemn moment in its history. The question was a simple one: Was the statement as it stood sufficiently strong, sufficiently clear? Ought not the note of conciliation to be strengthened?

They were all aware that certain forces in the nation were carrying out attacks on persons and institutions which they mistakenly felt were too committed to changes and reforms – reforms which he assumed those present agreed to be necessary. (Here the dark-suited technocrats nodded.) Some of these attacks had even been directed against priests and members of the hierarchy of the Church. Those responsible belonged to a tiny group whose name – the Guerillas of Christ the King – was an attempt to convince the devout Catholics of Spain that this anarchic behaviour had in some sense the blessing of the Church. What they were in effect intent on was keeping alive the great divisions which had so tragically rent the nation. Theirs was a backward-looking mentality, which was not in accord with the direction Spain must take almost half a century after those tragic days.

He was of the opinion, therefore, that the statement ought to state clearly how the Caudillo would have wished to define his enemies. Perhaps there might be a form of words that said something to the effect that 'he had had no enemies who were not also the enemies of Spain', that was to say, of the Spanish nation as a whole. As one who by the nature of his office had long been privy to the most intimate thoughts of the Caudillo, he wished with due deference to suggest to His Excellency and those assembled tonight that this formulation had the advantage of being in the nature of a gesture towards those who had fought on the opposing side in the most tragic war in the history of the Spanish people. The Caudillo, faced by the awful moment when he must face his Maker, would – he was sure – have wished to hold out an olive branch of forgiveness and reconciliation. The speaker ended with a deferential inclination of the head to the prelate, who said he found the formulation apt, expressing the spirit of reconciliation which it was the wish of the Church to foster in Christian forgiveness.

At the other end of the palace, the Carmelite nun was relieved by another sister. The hand-over was brief. A few low words. Nothing new. No change. Her way through the corridors to the street where the car waited to return her to the convent led her past the room where the meeting had passed on to a momentous decision which could no longer be deferred: the decision to allow the force of nature to take its course and the soul of the Caudillo to be received into the hands of God. A couple of guards on the door watched her pass swiftly along the corridor but she was barely aware of them, for out of long habit she kept her eyes cast down towards the floor. Just after she passed the decision had been taken. In two days' time the doctors would allow the Caudillo to die from natural causes. The death certificate would refer to miocardiac arrest, massive haemorrhaging, peritonitis, acute renal failure, thrombophlebitis, bronchial pneumonia, irremediable heart failure.

It was, Fergus comforted himself, a good sign that although he had been told to go back to his room, the door this time had not been locked from the outside. He would be able, they had told him, to get up, go to the bathroom and to the kitchen to drink or eat something – but first he must knock on the door and ask permission. Through the door he could still hear voices, no doubt continuing the discussion in which he had taken part.

The questions they would be running over were the same as those that preoccupied him now. How could he establish his credentials? What steps could they take to confirm his claims? Had they understood his explanations of the professional requirements that had led him to seek out and interview men who were the political and military leaders of right-wing militias funded and armed by the CIA? Would they accept his assurances that in screening footage shot in their mountain headquarters or in their villas in Miami he was not merely providing a platform for their views; that he had always tried to balance their statements with interviews from the other side – from his side – giving the comrades' case, explaining what they were fighting and dying for?

He had had to admit that the final editorial decision was not always his and that he sometimes had little or no control over the context in which his material used or in what terms it was discussed. But the comrades must understand – his comrades back home certainly did – that these were the hazards of his profession and that the risk was worth taking. And then there was the work he had done directly for the Party: in Nicaragua with the Sandinistas, for instance; in the Lebanon for the PLO; in South Africa (illicitly) for COSATU, which had relaxed the ban on visiting film-crews to allow him to shoot in the townships and to inter-view men and women outlawed by their racist govern-ment.

He had suggested that Judith be brought from the flat – where they had assured him she was safe and being looked after – to add her testimony to his. But they objected that she was one of the reasons for their suspicions, a co-worker and partner who was not a comrade. Was this not, to say the least of it, careless? But he was sure of Judith, he had replied. Now sitting on his bed, he was no longer so certain; she might quite simply be unco-operative. He could imagine her asking herself why she should help him out of a situ-ation he had managed to get himself into, against her advice and entreaties. Or she might simply be convinced that he was caught up in a web of paranoia. Even if she co-operated there was the problem that her evidence would not carry much weight with the comrades.

But who were these comrades? Not Stalinists, that was clear. Beyond that he was unsure, for he had never taken much interest in doctrinal distinctions on the Left. When he read the Party newspaper the articles he skipped were the ones given over to denunciations of heretics. So were they Maoists? Perhaps. Or some sort of Iberian variant drawing on the country's tradition of bombing – the tradition that had produced the *dinamiteros* of the Civil War, of the Astu-rian miners who hurled their bundles of short-fused explo-sives under the advancing Fascist tanks.

Certainly they were planning a bomb attack. On what? On whom? He remembered the tough line the Party had always taken about terrorism, dismissing it as petty bourgeois

115

romantic individualism which was no substitute for the harder, less spectacular work of raising the consciousness of the working class, acting as a vanguard that could lead them in their struggle against reaction wherever it was, whatever exact form it took. These were the differences, far-reaching and important ones, Comrade Fred had always said; but he had said, too, that solidarity could sometimes override them. It depended on the precise conjuncture, the exact moment in the struggle. After all, he would recall, the Bolsheviks had robbed banks after the defeat of the 1905 revolution. And why the hell not? But still, Fergus had doubts. Behind them lurked the darker suspicion that the 'comrades' might be *agents provocateurs*, leading him on for their own secret and ruthless ends.

So it was in a moment of desperation that when the meeting, the interrogation – whatever it had been – ended, he had reluctantly given the Don three telephone numbers. Reluctantly, because doubt niggled at him and because what he was doing was undoubtedly a breach of security. The numbers were that of the Boatyard. That of Comrade Fred at his flat, which very few comrades were allowed to know. That of Siobhan. Of these, the first two were certain to be bugged. If so, would the British secret services get in touch with their Spanish colleagues? Did such links exist? But then if the call was made from some main post office the caller could almost certainly get away before the call could be traced. The Don had promised to let him know the outcome of their inquiries sometime next morning.

The doubts kept Fergus from sleep far into the night but he still woke early and knocked dutifully on his door. There was no reply from the room beyond. Pushing the door ajar he looked out into the living-room. There was no one at the table on which lay a tool bag, some electrical wire and a pair of long-nosed pliers. No sign of the suitcase he had brought from Los Huertos. From another bedroom came snoring, which broke off from time to time as if the sleeper had lost the rhythm, stumbled as it were in his sleep. Whoever it was – Luis, presumably – did not stir at the noise Fergus made in bathroom or kitchen. It was still dark, dull and windy outside, cold. Foraging in a cupboard he found some *jamon* and a piece of not very fresh roll and began to eat. In the fridge there was a bottle of beer. He moved quietly and watched the sky pale.

He remembered how his father, who was full of what he alleged to be Highland folklore, had used to say that there was a point between day and night when death came more easily – just as it did at slack water when the tide was on the turn, full but about to ebb. It was this folksy crap that had used to set his teeth on edge. It had gone along with holidays spent tramping in a kilt through wet heather and knee-high bracken up the side of burns that petered out into squelching bogs, beyond which the ground rose and the real climb began. This was called going back to one's roots. At the end of it there would be a cairn where he would be commanded to add his stone as his father had before him as a boy. Back at the hotel he would cringe when his father, shaking the rain from his deerstalker, said audibly and apparently in all seriousness: 'My foot is on my native heath – my name's MacIver.'

In one of their moments of conspiratorial closeness which – though they never spoke of them – both knew was their haven from the man who dominated their lives, Fergus had asked his mother whether it was possible to change one's name. Yes, she had said, after all she had changed hers when she got married. No, that wasn't what he meant; did he have to go on being called Fergus Alpin MacIver? His mother had given him a slight hug and asked with a laugh why on earth he should want to change such a nice name. 'Oh you know, Mum,' he replied, 'you know. They make fun of me at school.' She hugged him again and he smelt the powder on her face. But she was silent. Silence, he knew, was her defence against the world. As he recalled that moment in the cold of the Madrid dawn he thought that it was no doubt with silence that she had responded to her husband's sexual advances – no crying out in orgasm but silence and perhaps a curious kind of affection, a little kiss or a slight touch of the hand as he turned away and slept.

Fergus had returned to the subject of his name several times, but she had refused to go along with his line of thought, had merely said these were things he could make up his mind about when he was grown-up. In the end it hadn't been worth the trouble, had ceased to matter. The name looked all right there in the credits, carried his professional authority and no one made fun of him any more – except Comrade Fred, who insisted on giving him his full name: Fergus Alpin MacIver. Mockingly, of course. Taking him down a peg. Letting him know that middle-class members were perhaps not to be taken seriously, had to prove themselves.

He wondered how he would be received at the Boatyard when he got back. He had no doubt that there would be some sort of inquest when he would have to come clean about the extra assignment, about the suitcase and his part in what he could not deny was a terrorist action. Would it be condemned as a piece of pure adventurism? He had not been present at one of the internal commissions which dealt with disciplinary matters but there were stories of Comrade Fred's rages or even worse of cold denunciations against which no defence was allowed. One comrade had said over a drink – but he had since left the Party – that it was like hearing a Wee Free minister denouncing a sinner. Not that he had ever heard a Wee Free minister but that was how he imagined them. Siobhan had remarked quietly that this was very remarkable since Comrade Fred had been brought up a Catholic.

Fortunately when Fergus was summoned to the Boatyard, just before what Comrade Fred referred to as 'your

Spanish trip', it was not to be denounced but to be made an offer. It was like this, Comrade Fred had said with a grin; the Party had had a sort of windfall. Where from? Never mind where from. People were going to wonder. Libya? Iraq? At least they wouldn't be able to say it was Moscow gold. Comrade Fred barked a short laugh. But he didn't give a tinker's. Wasn't there a saying that money doesn't stink? He had a feeling Marx quoted it somewhere. Anyway, he added with a wink, what was the Fighting Fund comrades and friends contributed to intended for if not to subsidize party activities? Well, one way and another there was enough in the kitty to buy a couple of professional film cameras with sound equipment and an editing table. What about that, eh? But to come to the point: was Comrade Fergus MacIver, whom a wee bird told him had a certain reputation in the field, willing to take on the film activities of the Party? He would get paid – at union rates naturally – but not full-time, of course. He'd still be able to do things for himself. So he should think it over – take his time – but think it over seriously. It was an important step for him professionally and for the Party. Comrade Fergus knew the Party's attitude to personal problems – sympathetic of course – but he also knew where his loyalty lay. With the party of the working class and with the revolution. Well, the comrade could give an answer when he got back. Mission accomplished and all that. And with a clap on the shoulder Comrade Fred had despatched him.

Ever since he had walked out of the big gates at the end of that interview, Fergus had been thinking it over. Trying to come to what must be a crucial decision. In the small world where he worked everyone would quickly know the set-up. People would distance themselves. It was very simple: producers wouldn't want to work with, be associated with him any more. There would be no need for a blacking (strenuously denied). The Corporation would be able to say, hand on its collective and bureaucratic heart, that

Fergus MacIver had not been blacked. They would naturally be more than willing to look at any projects he put forward on their merits. There would be whispers in canteens and bars that he was anyway just a little *passé*, a tiny bit old-fashioned, stuck in a tradition which had produced great stuff but was dated. 'You know what I mean, just a touch humourless, a bit dour, a bit worthy. Very John Grierson. A bit Scottish? Yes, a bit Scottish.'

A footstep behind him startled him, made him turn round. It was Luis, the young bomb-maker with the dark hair, broad shouldered, not pleased. Telling Fergus to get back into his room. Fergus shrugged and said: *No intiendo.* The young man left the kitchen and coming back with a handgun waved it about and pointed to the door. Fergus finished laying a couple of thin slices of *jamon* on a roll before he complied. He closed the door behind him. Listened. The key was not turned in the lock. That at least was progress of some kind.

In his room he walked up and down. Pulled open a drawer and looked at the old newspaper that thriftily lined it. There was a photograph of the dictator, smiling, accepting a bouquet from a child. He began to pace the room again, turning over the future in his mind. There was still Judith. If he took up Comrade Fred's offer – was it an offer or a veiled command? – that would mean the end as far as she was concerned. Theirs would not be the first or last relationship to founder on the demands made by the Party. He thought of the comrade with the gravelly voice who had become a full-time organizer, dispatched to Newcastle to recruit the youth, to harness the energies of the football fans behind the revolution, because, comrades, if we can get the working-class youth off the terraces and into the streets – not just rampaging and throwing beer-cans at the boys in blue but fighting on our side – we will be home and dry in the confrontations that lie before us as the rotten system falls apart. So the comrade had gone to Newcastle and from

Newcastle to a housing estate in Glasgow and his wife had packed up, taken the children and gone off as far away as possible to live with her mother in New Zealand. Like her, Judith would not tolerate the régime the party would impose, the long hours, the sudden assignments, the secrecy and mysteries. And there would be no question of his being allowed to use her as a researcher, no way in which she would be allowed through the huge Boatyard gates. But all this was in the uncertain future; for the moment he was more concerned with the problem of how he could get in touch with her. For two reasons. She had the tickets and their flight was the day after tomorrow. He would make a demand when the Don turned up. Then once they were back in London they could try to find out whether there was a chance of patching something up, of finding a way of living together that drew on all that he and she found positive, reassuring – companionship, love – whatever you cared to call it. They had really and finally come to a turning point, he thought, as he lay on the bed and waited for what the grey November day might bring.

When she woke, Judith decided she would insist that Pilar arrange for her to talk to Fergus. She had checked the ticket in the inner pocket of her big leather bag. The flight was at noon in two days' time. If the worst came to the worst she would wait till Pilar opened the front door to go shopping, which she seemed to do daily, push her aside, slip past and make a run for it. Pilar was in no state to catch her. There must be a bus to the city centre and then a taxi to take her to the airport. She could hang about there until the plane left, even if it meant sleeping on a bench in the departure lounge a couple of nights. She would leave the other ticket on the dressing-table where Pilar would see it and perhaps some-how get it to Fergus. It would be up to him to use it or not. She could, she felt, do no more and no less. There seemed no way in which she could extricate him – provided he wanted to be extricated – from a situation which was obscure to her though surely dangerous. But it was precisely the danger that drew him on.

She had tried to talk about it – about his fascination with danger and risk – to her therapist, her counsellor, but he had turned her questions aside saying that they were there to discuss her problems and not those of her partner who might be well advised to discuss them with some qualified person. Really all they could do was try to find out why she felt unable to assert herself in the relationship and lay down certain parameters, certain ground rules which were agreed and observed by both sides. Should that prove impossible, she might have to consider what she felt about the relationship – how valuable it was to her, what she got out of it, why she felt she must persist in it. He was not suggesting any particular action to her, merely inviting her to think about it as clearly as possible. Lying in this shuttered room in some unknown suburb of Madrid, Judith decided that she had achieved clarity.

She found Pilar in her dressing-gown making coffee. 'I want to talk to my friend,' she said. Pilar poured her a cup and pushed it towards her, shaking her head. 'I'm sorry,' she said, 'I don't know the number. They won't tell me. They can phone me. I can't phone them.'

'Fuck,' said Judith. Pilar laughed and imitated her. 'That's one word I know,' she said and went on in curiously aspirated English. 'You want fuck. It cost you one thousand pesetas.' She laughed again. 'Do you know the Spanish for "fuck"?' '*Chingar*,' said Judith, the word Sebastian had conjugated in all its tenses and forms in the course of their long, bitter process of separation. After a wide-eyed pause Pilar went on: 'I don't know where you learned it but I learned to say it in English at Chicote's. You learn a lot when you work in a place like that. Not just words. About men who agree a price and then try to cheat you. Who accuse you of stealing their money. Who blame you when they can't get it up. Who want you to be a mother, a lover, or God knows what. Who want something – they don't know what it is and they're never going to find out. But they seem to think a woman has it between her legs. They are the dangerous ones because if they are disappointed, if they don't find whatever it is they are looking for, they can turn into killers. One of them killed a friend of mine, a girl from Chicote's. We had a saying that what they were really in love with was death. Women should be careful of men in love with death. Have you ever met one?'

Judith was silent.

'Manuel wasn't like that. Even though he was a *torero*. He got tired of me in the end. Found this young woman in Malaga, they tell me. But when we were together he was good and generous and didn't want me to be anything but what I was. But my son now – he was one of them, I think. He talked a lot, but I didn't understand much of it – about the fight for the class and for some International or other, whatever that is. But you don't have to be in love with death to fight for justice. My father wasn't. He would have been happy to go on driving his tram. Lying in bed with my mother, fucking' (Pilar used the word with a smile of complicity) 'during the siesta. I used to hear them. But he fought in University City. My mother wasn't either. She fought too. But she didn't want to die and when they came to take her from the cell she held on to me and wept but they pulled her away. We were all women there. Weeping, praying. Then we heard the volleys in the courtyard where they shot people. In batches. She wasn't in love with death. Nor am I. I don't want to die but I do want to avenge my son. What about you? What about your father?'

Judith shook her head. She had no answer. What she had always imagined was that he had gone to Spain on the orders of the Party – but how had he gone? In sorrow, parting tearfully from his pregnant wife on the platform at Victoria? Or in excitement, drawn by some deep desire that was more exciting than sex – those unimaginable couplings in love and desire in which she, Judith, must have been conceived? Something that was hidden behind the dream of a better, more just society in which people would live in peace and plenty? She knew about that dream because she had heard Sebastian's father and his Republican friends talking about it in Roman bars and cafés with Italian comrades, ageing men of their own generation who had fought for the same cause in the International Brigades in Spain and after that in the Resistance in Italy. But by the time she got to know them they were living on their past, telling stories over and over again in which certain names recurred and fell into place in the history she had been attempting to put together since her adolescence – names like University City, Jarama, Albacete.

At first she had listened with interest; then she had become bored by stories shaped and polished by endless repetition – troubled, too, by what she detected as boastful exaggerations and even more by a vein of cruel humour: laughter at the memory of how a comrade having a shit in an olive grove had been wounded in the arse by a piece of shrapnel and, of course, the story about the frozen Moor. Then there was the way they smirked like naughty schoolboys over visits to the brothels of Albacete until they suddenly remembered her presence and the talk died in a moment of embarrassment that someone broke with a laugh and a word or two of excuse. Sometimes boredom, puzzlement and revulsion made her tug at Sebastian's sleeve and say 'Let's go home', but he would shake his head impatiently and later they would quarrel and his conjugation of *chingar* would begin. She was fed up, she said, with having to sit through the same routine night after night – yes, she was fed up – and while she was at it she would thank him not to introduce her to people by saying that her father had fought in the International Brigade. She was herself, a person in her own right, she would end up shouting, not just the daughter of a dead man with the right political credentials. That was a burden she had borne long enough.

'I thought maybe I would learn about him by coming to Spain,' she said at length.

'And have you?'

Judith considered.

'I don't know,' she said.

Pilar came over and gave her a hug.

'Have you ever wept for him? He was a young man – how old – twenty-six? Young men like him, they are buried all over Spain. But their graves are forgotten, covered over, bulldozed. No one knows who they were. Why don't you just weep for him and leave him behind you here in Spain? Stop being angry with a dead man. You can't go on being angry for the rest of your life.'

'But you're angry,' said Judith.

Pilar shrugged.

'That's different. I've something to be angry about. Even though the man who signed my son's death warrant is dying. I can't help hoping he is suffering. But they'll make sure he doesn't suffer too much. I know what it will be like – him lying there with the nuns and the nurses and doctors and his wife and daughter. He won't know much about it, except maybe when the priest performs the last rites. Maybe not even then. But that's not the same – is it? – as being a young man or a young woman – like my mother was – tired maybe, afraid, but fit, alive, knowing all the time what is happening to you and having to walk out of a cell into the courtyard and see the black posts with the squad standing there and wait for the command, Fire! I wonder sometimes whether they heard the word, or was there just one terrible noise and then nothing more?

'I'd like to be able to pay that man back for those moments.

But I know I can't. I know that. And the friends of Carlos know it, too – the men who got the stuff you brought from Los Huertos. The most they can do is to blow up some official car, one of those dark ones with the special number plates that drive about this city as if they owned it; get at whoever's sitting in it in his dark suit and grey tie, someone who ran that man's errands and listened to his boring speeches and crept to him and carried in the sheaf of death sentences to be signed. But I know nothing will be changed. A fart in the face of the men of power – that's all. So Carlos' friends will do their best. As for me, I'll hear about it on the radio, or maybe there will be pictures in television. And I will feel a little less angry. In any case when the man dies I shall get together with *las chicas* and we'll celebrate with a bottle or two of champagne.' Pilar paused and reflected, her face set and expressionless.

'The last time it happened,' she said, 'they showed on television how the car had been blown right over the roof of the ministry and into the courtyard behind. Did they show it on your television? Someone told me it had been seen all over the world. A lot of people here were frightened. I was frightened for my son. They took him a week later. The day before they shot him I went out to Carabanchel. But he didn't want to see me. I could understand that. It would have been too difficult for him. He wanted to be left to himself. Like the bull when it's near the end and there is only it and the *torero* in the ring together. Have you ever been to a *corrida*? No? Well, the bulls – they choose a space in the ring and fight and die there. There's a special word for it: *la querencia*. So my son didn't want anyone to come into the space where he had to face death.'

She stopped talking and, stretching out a leg knotted with veins, massaged an ankle reflectively.

'There's one difference, though, between me and Carlos' friends. I am willing to help them because I have a reason. A reason of my own. I want to settle scores because of my

126

son. I have never wanted to kill anyone before. I'll never want to again. But they're different. They want to kill for a cause. That means they will go on killing. First this one and then that one. I am frightened of men who kill for a cause. You never know where they will stop. You never know when you will become an enemy, be put on a list, rubbed out. To kill once because there is nothing else you can do, because it is the only thing that makes sense to you as a woman. That is one thing, but to kill for a cause is bad.'

Then she fell silent. The day crept past. There were no phone calls that morning. Pilar was silent and contemplative. A shadow swept in an arc over the floor as they sat in silence. In the afternoon Pilar disappeared to her room. Judith, too, went to lie on her bed and face the tedious emptiness of the two hours of the siesta. Was Pilar perhaps her Wise Woman, she wondered. Why had she never been able to weep for the man called Tony Gordon? Why had the South African who was so cool in his knowledge never offered her the relief of tears? But suppose she did weep, what would she be weeping for? She had not wept since the phone-call that told her that Kev had died. But those had been tears for a real loss – loss of fun, of his company, of sex. But now? She turned the pillow which was hot under her cheek, but her eyes were dry. What miracle would make them spring and from what source?

When she rose, Pilar was already in the room where she lived and cooked and watched television. She was sitting at the table over which she had spread a cloth. On it were laid out a handgun and a magazine into which Pilar was deftly feeding bullets from a little cardboard box.

'Have you ever seen one of these?' Pilar asked. 'I got it from Manuel. I used to think of going to Malaga and shooting him. But in the end it seemed too much trouble. I suppose I had got over him.'

127

She held the pistol out to Judith, who took it in her hand. It was quite small and fitted easily into her grasp. The metal was blueish. In the muzzle there was a hole, an orifice, not exactly erotic but troubling – as if she were looking at something from which decency should have made her avert her eyes. She thought of a medieval image of Satan – seen where? in some Italian gallery? in Siena maybe – a sexually ambiguous figure with breasts, dugs rather, and between its legs an orifice that was neither anus nor vagina but something more and different: a hole from which the filth of evil flowed. She was, she felt, looking at the orifice of death and laid the gun down on the table with a gesture of revulsion that made her rub her hands on her jeans.

'I want you to have it,' said Pilar. 'Come. I'll teach you.'

Reluctantly Judith drew a chair up to the table. Pilar explained the mechanism. Showed her how to charge the magazine, pushing the rounds – so small it hardly seemed that they could kill a person – down against the resistance of the spring. Demonstrated how easily the magazine went home. Flicked the safety catch on and off. Removed the magazine and showed how the cocking mechanism slid to and fro, how to put pressure on the trigger. Judith took the gun up and felt its weight, its balance, how it became an extension of her arm just as Kev's equipment had seemed to become a part of his body. She laid it down again with a sudden gesture that spoke of fear but Pilar took it up and held it to her, butt first.

'Don't be silly,' she said. 'Take it. It's a good gun. Handy. A Beretta. Made in Italy. Put it in that big bag of yours. You never know.'

Reluctantly Judith took it up again and carried it back to her bedroom. Sitting on the bed she withdrew the magazine and pulled back the cocking mechanism. There was a fascination in the way the steel parts moved, smoothly, surely, in the slight click as some part of the mechanism moved into place. She put her finger on the trigger, felt the resistance of the spring and how the firing mechanism responded when she pressed harder. She went through the process two or three times, admiring the smoothness of the action as if it were part of some innocent piece of equipment. Suddenly she remembered one of her PenWar notes and how her rifleman wrote calmly from the safety of memory:

I can distinctly remember the sharp crashing sound of a bullet which striking a steady old sergeant in the centre of his forehead pierced his brain.

Hurriedly she picked her big leather bag off the floor and thrust the gun deep inside. At the bottom it was rendered safe, as it were, innocuous among the odds and ends of her daily life. When she went back, Pilar said nothing.

It was after they had eaten their evening meal and the television was flickering with a blueish light in the corner of the room with the sound turned down that the telephone rang. Pilar answered. Then without a word she held the receiver out to Judith.

The voice at the other end was Fergus's. Cool, feigning normality.

'Hi, it's me,' it said, 'how have you been?'

The idiot, thought Judith, how does he think I've been? Her reply was a minimal, uncommunicative 'OK. And you?'

'A spot of bother you might call it. They've been taking up my references. But it looks as if some misunderstandings had been cleared up.'

'So?' she began restraining a surge of hope.

'I can't really discuss –'

His voice was cut off and another took its place. Not a young voice which said in good but accented English:

'Someone will pick you later. A friend of Carlos. Be ready.'

The phone clicked as the line went dead.

'Well?' said Pilar.

'They are going to pick me up.'
Pilar said nothing.

It was dusk when the bell rang from the main entrance and Pilar went to the answerphone, cautious, suspicious, requiring some sort of password or recognition.

A young man came in, whom Judith did not think she had seen before. 'Where are you taking her?' said Pilar. The young man looked at her coldly and said he knew what he had to do: pick up the *Inglesita* and deliver her. He had nothing to tell Pilar. Meantime the *Inglesita* had better hurry and get her things together. To be honest he had expected something a bit younger, a bit sexier. To Judith's amazement, Pilar slapped the man across the face and told him to talk decently. The *señorita* spoke Castilian better than he did who was nothing but a peasant from Murcia. The man swore but it was more politely that he told Judith to get ready to come with him. All she took was her big leather bag, which she slung over one shoulder. It felt much heavier than before. Pilar gave her a hug and kissed her on both cheeks. 'Good luck,' she said standing in the hallway. Her face had resumed the mask-like quality that had struck Judith when first they met. '*Que tengas suerte,*' she said again as if to wish her good fortune twice over might make it easier for Judith to confront the uncertainties of the night.

The young man drove in silence. The streets were almost empty, as if the city's inhabitants were waiting indoors for something, some voice, some clangour of bells, some signal to announce that these great squares would never again be filled by the supporters of the man who had ruled for more than thirty years. Waiting in fear and uncertainty, in expectation and excitement, with the sense that they were living through one of those moments that are marked off in history, circled on calendars, celebrated or mourned. But in narrow streets whores stood in entrances or sauntered along

along the pavements and men paired off with them to disappear into dark doorways that led to dim passages and stairs. '*Putas*,' said the young man redundantly, as if he were pointing out some landmark, some guide-book entry. Judith said nothing.

They had passed through the city centre and were now moving into a suburb where flats were solid, comfortable. In some windows there was a flickering light where the inhabitants sat round their television sets. They stopped in a side street, residential, quiet. The door was quickly opened to them. The hallway reminded Judith of certain old-fashioned flats in Rome – uncomfortable, with solid, dark furniture ranged against the walls. In the living-room there was Fergus, sitting at a long table. He rose when she came in and kissed her on the cheek. She was uncertain what to do. 'Sit down, please,' said a man in his fifties or early sixties with a long thin face and greying hair, who might have been anything from a lawyer to an academic or civil servant. His English was good. As she sat down she could feel the handgun bump against her thigh. There were four men including Fergus, who had taken his place at the other end of the table as if to distance himself from her, looking pale but composed. As she caught his eye he gave a slight smile that was meant to reassure her. The other two men were younger. One was dressed conventionally. He had a face from which she recognized the genetic inheritance of the ancient people of the Americas. The other wore a leather jacket, was dark and slightly nervous, twisting a piece of wire between his fingers.

'*Bueno*, said the eldest of them, 'we have to talk.'

Through the day there had already been a good deal of talking. Luis, the young man with the leather jacket, had taken no part for he had been busy with the contents of the suitcase and with the intricacies of wiring the charges of explosives to a timer – an ordinary alarm clock, it seemed to Fergus. But occasionally he would pause in his work and look over to where Fergus sat opposite the Don, discussing terrorism. Why? To pass the time, to fill the anxious void in which Fergus felt he was suspended, in an attempt to establish his credentials as a man of the Left. But he knew it was pointless. Anyone could learn the language and its vocabulary. Fergus remembered an interpreter in Honduras who had gone on in erudite detail about the factions of the Fourth International. Then someone had warned Fergus that he was in fact a CIA agent. Maybe he was, maybe he wasn't. But who knew? At all events he disappeared without explanation. There were, Fergus knew, spaces, black holes, down which people could disappear, sucked away by the tempest of history, of the revolution, of the unforgiving struggle.

At any rate he and the Don talked. He raised no objection when Fergus called him Quijote but that, too, meant nothing. A guard can permit himself to be goodnatured – he has the power. From time to time the Don would give Luis what Fergus guessed was a translation of the gist of their discussion. In mid-morning he broke off and went out. He was away for about half an hour, during which Fergus speculated whether anyone had made contact with London yet through a third party, talked to a Spanish comrade in London who in turn would call Comrade Fred or Comrade Siobhan. He imagined the phone ringing in the room that looked out on the private garden or by the bed in which he and Siobhan had lain and talked and made love. But suppose they were away – speaking in the north, at a weekend school – or suppose they were diffident, suspicious, requiring proofs of identity before they would part with information about a comrade who was on a mission to Spain? And even supposing the answer from London was positive – which it must be – and that he was, so to speak, cleared, there would still have to be some sort of consultation about what was to happen to him next – and to Judith. If the answer was unsatisfactory there might, he feared, be consultations of a different sort.

At last the Don returned, with a newspaper under his arm. 'Comrade,' said Fergus, 'can I ask what is happening?' The Don looked at him and tossed on to the table *El Diario Nuevo*. 'We are making enquiries,' he said and pushed the paper over to Fergus, who mechanically picked it up. He could decipher some of the editorial. It seemed to be saying that the great man – who was still mentioned with the honorifics of the dictatorship – should be allowed to die in peace, not kept alive artificially for reasons of state. 'They will let him die soon,' said the Don. 'He has ceased to be useful to them.' Then he took up the thread of their conversation where Fergus had left off.

He had been defining his stance and the stance of his party, which saw terrorism as a petty-bourgeois attempt to solve a political situation by some exemplary act, some blow struck at one of the highest figures in the land. A romantic gesture. But what did that change? The system was left intact. The police and secret services were alerted and strengthened. There was the danger of a round-up of men and women on the Left, so that results of the long slow task of forming networks and cells, of recruiting forces and training cadres for the decisive moment – for a wave of demonstrations and strikes to rally the working class and its allies was dissipated. The networks destroyed. Important cadres imprisoned or forced into hiding where they were neutralized. In short it was a romantic, quixotic tactic.

Looking across with a slight smile to where the young comrade snipped at a piece of wire, the Don suddenly said that perhaps it was by being both quixotic and successful – as well as being fifty years old with a coarse complexion and, what was the expression? a wizened face – that he had earned his nom-de-guerre.

There was a slight pause during which Luis rose and

came back from the kitchen with coffee. As they drank, the Don was thoughtful. They ought, he said at last, to get back to the matter in hand. Fergus had certainly given the classic analysis of terrorism, but there was always a danger in applying analyses made at one conjuncture to other very different situations. There were cases where an exemplary act was necessary; it could be the match that lit the fuse of revolt. That was the situation he and his comrades faced. So Fergus and his comrades back in London might find it quixotic. But they did not face quite the same problems as their comrades here in Spain where, in any case, there was a long and honourable tradition of terrorism. He feared that Fergus and his comrades might be in danger of adopting a Stalinist stance, a kind of legalism which could be an excuse for avoiding revolutionary action.

Suddenly he changed tack to enquire whether Fergus had ever had to use a false name, to work in illegality. Fergus shook his head. Not in illegality in the sense of being part of an underground, although he had occasionally used a code-name when conducting negotiations with persons and organizations when it was inadvisable for one reason or another to give his real name. In case someone let it out. Had he ever used the code-name Ferdinando? Fergus shook his head. There had often been difficulties with his name and sometimes he had gone along with it when in Honduras or Guatemala they had transformed it into its nearest Spanish equivalent. But he could not recall using it specifically as a code-name. The comrade looked at him quizzically and merely commented, 'The comrade from Guatemala thinks you did.'

At that their conversation came to a halt. There followed a long exchange between the two Spanish comrades during which, it seemed to Fergus, in a studied way they avoided looking at him. Or was he merely yielding to paranoia, to what he knew could be a fatal blurring of judgement – something to be avoided, strenuously avoided. But he

134

was unable to repress a feeling of anxiety when at a ring of the door bell the young man got up and let in the dark-complexioned comrade whom he now knew was from Guatemala. At a gesture from him the Don rose, and together they disappeared into the kitchen.

Luis returned to his usual place at the table and started to pack his explosives into what looked like a shoe-box. Fergus concentrated on watching the deft movement of his fingers. From the kitchen he could detect the rise and fall of the two voices. It ceased as the two men came back into the room. The dark young man showed nothing in his face but the older comrade was smiling: 'Well, comrade,' he said, 'you are in the clear. AOK as the Americans say.' And he shook Fergus by the hand. Fergus could only say 'Ah – right', aware of a rush of warmth over his whole body, an outbreak of sweat like the crisis of a fever. 'That's good.' 'Yes,' said the Don, 'it's good. You were going to be a problem otherwise. Meantime we have to have a serious discussion.'

Even before he heard the details, Fergus recognized that what was being proposed to him was a crucial test; he was being asked to gamble deliberately, consciously, on the highest stakes. The word from London, the Don explained, was that Fergus was in the clear – a comrade – and they were grateful to him for delivering the stuff, *los chismos*. Hearing the word, Luis looked up from fiddling with his equipment and grinned. So far so good. But they wanted to put a suggestion to him which naturally he did not have to accept, to put it to him in terms of an appeal to his revolutionary conscience. There was no disguising that there were certain differences between the comrades in Spain and those in London. But what they were asking for was critical solidarity at a crucial moment in the Spanish struggle. The comrade must by now have a fair idea of the operation they were involved in, which was (parenthetically) why difficult decisions would have had to be made had his clearance not come through. The question was this: Was he prepared to take the operation a step further forward? There was naturally no compulsion but the comrades in charge of the operation believed he could make a valuable contribution to its success. Why? Because he was presumably unknown to the authorities, to the police, to the Seguridad. If he agreed to become involved, this was what it would entail.

By the end of the afternoon they had worked out the details, had studied street maps, calculated timings. It was a long discussion. As a kind of postscript, Fergus proposed a bargain. He wanted his partner to be brought over. He would vouch for her silence and would guarantee that she would respect certain limitations on her freedom of movement. They would leave together on the morning plane the day after the operation. They already had tickets.

There was first a silence and then a longish exchange between Don Quijote and the Guatemalan comrade, who was clearly raising objections. Luis took no part. He was putting the final touches to the wiring, snipping the end of a wire, testing a circuit. At last the discussion ended. 'All right,' said the Don, 'but she is your responsibility. And we are not playing games.' The phone was on a table in the corner of the room, a surprisingly old-fashioned instrument. The Don dialled a number, spoke briefly and then handed the receiver to Fergus, who could think of nothing better to say than 'Hi, it's me, how have you been?' He only had time to pass on a minimum of information when the Don took the receiver from his hand and said a friend of Carlos would come to fetch her. Then he put down the receiver.

There was a curious silence for a moment that no one seemed able or anxious to fill. Luis had closed the suitcase and sat with one hand resting on the lid. Then the Don proposed a toast and they drank to the success of the operation, to the downfall of Fascism and to the revolution.

What made Judith prickly, ready to be unco-operative, was the exaggerated courtesy with which this man in his fifties with his conventional dark grey suit, his thinning straight hair combed carefully from a parting on the left, his gaunt face and pale expression – as if the light had not got at it for a long time – addressed her. It spoke to her of a deep hypocrisy, for it was a kind of good manners, of tact, a way of treating her that went with a deep contempt for women, a conviction that they were creatures that had to be handled with care (at least in social intercourse) because otherwise they might prove incalculable, liable to outbursts of emotion, of anger or weeping. Hysterical, in short. It was a kind of politeness that would not prevent this gentleman – this comrade of Fergus's – from being a client at Chicote's, accustomed to treating today's Pilars with essential coldness as he bargained for access to their bodies and purchased it. No doubt even in those circumstances he would be reasonably polite, buy the girls a drink, perhaps exchange a few words with them about what – Real Madrid perhaps? Or where one of them had been on holiday, because he hadn't seen her for a week or two?

So it was with suspicion that she listened as he addressed her as señorita and complimented her on '*su dominio del castellano*'. All right, she said to herself, refusing to smile at his compliment, so I am fluent in Spanish, but why doesn't he come to the point? The other two men had mustered her as she came into the room. She was accustomed to the process, that scanning of her body, her legs, her breasts, the motion of her hips, the attention they paid to the way she sat down and crossed her legs. It was one of the irritations to which she was routinely subject. She decided to disregard them and to pay attention only to the older man, who was now with tactful circumlocutions explaining that it had been decided, at the specific request of the comrade from London, that it would be best if she were to stay here – it was a very safe house – until the day after tomorrow when along with the comrade she could take their scheduled morning flight back to London. She looked questioningly at Fergus but he was clearly in some way subservient to this man, who was empowered – with the power of the Cause, the Party, the International.

'Well?' she said.

'We've talked it through very thoroughly, the comrades and myself,' said Fergus, 'and they agreed to my request. So you can wait here till we fly out.'

'But I don't want to wait here. I want to go to a hotel. You can do what you want. It's up to you.'

The older man broke in. His charm was gone. His air and voice decisive. 'I am sorry,' he said, 'there can be no question of that. We have taken a decision. There can be no further discussion. You will stay here.'

In the bedroom the bed was unmade. Fergus made a quick, awkward attempt to straighten the sheets and plump up the pillows. Judith watched him in silence. It was in silence, too, that she undressed with the kind of shielded modesty she might have employed with a stranger, someone with whom an extraordinary chance had forced to share a room and a bed. Fergus asked: 'Are you all right?' to which she answered with a curt 'No'. Climbing into bed she drew the clothes up to her neck, turned her back to him. She felt the mattress shift a little under his weight, drew the clothes tighter round her and stretched her legs out in the cold sheets. He was there a few inches from her; she made no attempt to bridge the gap. Nor did he, lying still and, she could tell from his breathing, wide awake. Suddenly she felt a wave of fatigue sweep over her and, putting her nose under the sheet as she had used to do as a child to make sleep come, she let it engulf her.

She woke in the strange dark room. To find escape again she was tempted to turn and, putting her arm round Fergus, to let the accustomed warmth of his back soothe her to sleep. But she resisted the temptation. This man who lay next to her was – had made himself – a stranger of whom she could not ask for such closeness and comfort. For a time she studied the pattern the light coming through the slats of the persiennes made on the ceiling, listened for some sound in the house or from outside; but the window gave on to the silence of a courtyard in which nothing stirred. Once she thought she heard, very far away, a police or ambulance siren and the noise of cars in the empty streets. Then she slept again.

It was in the early morning that the doctors and their assistants in white coats came for the great man. The nun from Los Huertos stood up when they entered. But they disregarded her tentative gesture of help. Quickly, deftly, they disconnected tubes and electrodes, leaving only a drip that ran from a plastic flask to the needle fixed in the great man's arm. The nun caught a glimpse of his face, which was sunken and pale, and thought she saw a flicker, a tiny movement of the eyelids, a twitch of a cheek-muscle; but it might have been merely the way the shadow one of those angels of death fell as they went about their work. They moved the great man from the bed to a trolley and covered all but his face with a white sheet. She had seen deaths before but there was something in their silent dexterity that frightened her; their haste to remove him as if he were already some sort of waste, an offensive lump of flesh, that had to be disposed of. Then with only the almost imperceptible fall of rubber-soled shoes and the slight rumble of rubber wheels, they swept out of the room. She followed them to the door and watched as almost running – one at the head, another at the feet and a third at the side holding high the flask for the drip – they went down the long corridor and vanished through a side entrance to avoid the crowds she had seen as she came on duty early in the evening. She had no doubt that they would still be there, telling their beads, holding up their crucifixes, praying to the Mother of God to intercede for the dying man – *nunc et in hora* – their voices fusing into a single murmur that rose and fell in familiar cadences.

It was still dark when Fergus rose without waking Judith, who had moved slightly in the night so that he had felt the warmth of her body against his. Now before he left the room he covered her back and shoulder with the sheet. It was an automatic gesture which he had made often in the morning when he slipped from her side to catch an early flight and embark on an assignment that might carry him into cities where snipers had made their lairs deep in the jumbled ruins. It had usually meant a separation but one from which he would return to a kind of sharing, a closeness which was, he had decided – and it seemed she had, too – the next best thing to love. But that closeness had been eroded. Once back in London, the break would become final. But that it was already accomplished he knew as he shut the bedroom door quietly behind him. In the room where the council of war had been held the night before the glasses had been cleared from the long table and the ash-trays emptied. He opened the door to the kitchen, which was also unusually tidy. The comrades were taking steps to remove all traces of their presence. Once Judith and he had left all signs of occupation would be obliterated and the house would once again be gloomily empty and respectable, waiting for the lawyers to disentangle a will, to settle some problem of probate. At this early hour it was cold and depressing.

As Fergus walked up and down the length of the room he was clear in his mind that – if all went well – he would accept Comrade Fred's offer. Find somewhere to live. Anywhere. Put his skills at the disposal of the Party, bury himself in work. Train other comrades to make films wherever people fought against oppression, hunger, exploitation. Forget about sex. Go back to his Wise Woman clandestinely, for Comrade Fred, who made a laughing exception of Siobhan on the grounds that she was Irish and slightly fey, dismissed the kind of counsel she gave as witchcraft for the bourgeoisie.

The Wise Woman knew, of course, that he was politically committed but he had so far contrived to avoid any inquiry into the deep roots of that involvement. That would have led him into the painful territory where Oedipus was king, a tyrant who from beyond his ridiculous whisky-sodden death still held over him the rod he had been obliged to kiss and embrace as a child – a rod (he would have had to confess) handed on to the Party and wielded by Comrade Fred who chastised and bullied, damned and praised, expelled prodigals and welcomed them back, fucked their women in true Oedipal fashion and spoke with the authority of the sacred texts. These were, he knew, dangerous and deviant thoughts which would earn him more than some scoffing remarks from Siobhan, who had set herself up as the St Joan of the Party. They could have him expelled from the safety of the cutting-room where, using the dialectic of montage, he would create new meanings out of images he had found or captured and, secure in his professional skills, would dare to contradict Comrade Fred and his untutored judgements.

Perhaps when he saw his Wise Woman it would be safer to avoid the term of the Oedipal equation and concentrate instead on the figure of his mother. Explore how far she stood behind the woman he had lain beside, lain with, to whom he brought an offering of love to exchange for something ill-defined, something his mother had perhaps had it in her power to give him when she held him to her breast, sheltering him from the wrath of the man with the bayonet scar and the whisky-red face. But she had made him draw back out of fear of the King, out of alarmed awareness of her son's sexuality which had led him secretly to investigate her wardrobe and the drawers of her dressing-table, turning over her underwear, her nightdresses, her silk stockings, feeling their texture, holding them to his face, sniffing at them in the hope of tracing the source of the perfume, the slightly pungent aroma that rose from her body. It was a desire to discover these same secrets, to explore what lay beneath a woman's elaborate defences, to explore those secret places that promised softness and warmth that had driven him ever since his adolescence.

After Siobhan he had talked round and round his longing and as he talked and the Wise Woman listened, he was fleetingly, alarmingly aware, that he was allowing himself to look at her with the same interest, wondering what she might be like in bed, what the springs of her desire might be, what lay behind the calm neutrality she presented as he described how he had experienced miracles of touch and texture, cliff-edges of pleasure and pain, but how when the mutual explorations were over there had been a sense not of disappointment, rather of anti-climax, a feeling that there should have been at the end something else, some sort of unproblematic heaven.

Instead – 'Instead what?' she had asked. 'You told me once,' she went on, 'about some soft porn magazine you saw – and used – didn't you? – when you were sixteen – seventeen?' 'Yes,' he said and laughed, '*Silk Stocking* – the sort of thing you could see in any fashion magazine these days. Maybe what is or isn't sexually exciting isn't fixed for all time but is socially conditioned.' 'Maybe,' she said, but went on to say that they weren't there to discuss the erotic, fascinating as that might be. She wanted to suggest instead that he should be asking himself why he seemed to find it so difficult to cope not with some long-legged, silk-

142

stockinged doll but with real women, endowed not only with sexual power but with real problems, real needs, real demands of their own. Had he thought why he couldn't deal with them on equal terms, as one adult with another? Satisfy their emotional demands? Understand that they, too, might have needs? The thought of having to go back and wrestle with these old conundrums dismayed him. What had drawn him to Judith had been more than anything else companionship, shared interests, shared professional lives, mutual support. Sex, of course, yes, but it was the support that mattered. Which was what she was now withdrawing. But at least he would – with luck – be able to say (once the day that lay before him was safely over) that he no longer felt the need to wager his life, to vie in some obscure way with the man who had survived the killing-grounds of the Somme and in middle age had fucked his mother.

All this he would tell her if things went well, as they could hardly fail to do. His part was to drive the car he had hired – it was clean, its registration number presumably figured on no police list – to the little church where Goya was buried under a dome for which he had himself painted the frescos. Not many people visited it. Certainly not in November. Nearby was a space where he could park the car. Luis would be waiting there. Fergus would get out, leaving the key in the ignition. Then without looking back he would walk over to the church and go in as if to see the frescos. He would emerge after a decent interval and, checking to make sure he was not being tailed, walk up a steep path and a long flight of steps through a park to the Gran Via. Then back by public transport to the safe house.

It was all very simple. By the time he got back the operation would be successfully concluded. The next morning he and Judith could take their plane. They would be home by noon. He would see her back to her flat, get some of his things together and take the tube down to the Boatyard where there was a room for comrades who had to stay on when a meeting, called to hammer out some change in the Party line, lasted far into the night. He would be able to lodge there for a couple of days at least while he looked around for a place.

Yet there were naturally risks. Fergus turned them over in his mind. What if the car he had hired was known to the police? He had no idea where it had been kept since he and Judith arrived in the city. Presumably in some safe garage; but the security forces might have routinely noted the number when they stopped the car at the road-block outside the city. Might be ready to pounce when they thought the moment was right. There could be more road-blocks and inspections. He had managed to pass things off when he and Judith were driving in from Los Huertos. They had been lucky. But would he be lucky a second time? What should he do if challenged? Drive on and risk a burst of fire from a sub-machine gun? Perhaps if he spotted the road-block in time he might be able to turn up a side street. But then what? There would be no chance to consult his street map. And then how stable was the bomb? The comrades had assured him that it was absolutely safe. The timing mechanism was very accurate and there was no chance that it would go off prematurely.

As he contemplated the possibilities, he was aware of a sudden pang of fear which he mastered by relaxing, calming his heart. At least he was not running the same risk as the comrade who would take over in the parking place and drive down through the great avenues of the city to a rendezvous with the Minister in his black official car. If he kept his nerve, if the timing was right, the tyrant would be attended in death by one of his most faithful servants.

When Judith came out of the bedroom, she did not address

144

him but made her way to the bathroom. He went into the kitchen and looked for coffee. Hearing her emerge, he told her it would be ready soon, adding apologetically that the cupboard seemed to be bare. But maybe supplies would come later. She halted long enough in the doorway to hear him out and then without a word went into the bedroom and closed the door. When she came out again she was wearing her coat and had her big leather bag slung over her shoulder.

'I'm going to find a hotel,' she announced.

'You can't,' he said.

'Why can't I?'

'Because I promised.'

'Promised what?'

'That you'd stay here. Till tomorrow morning.'

'Promised whom?'

'The comrades.'

'But I didn't.' She began to walk towards the door. 'Who the hell gave you permission to answer for me anyway? I'm not playing your games any more.'

'It's not a game. It's serious.'

'I know,' she said. 'That's why I am going.'

'You can't,' he said, and moved quickly to the end of the table to cut her off.

She put her hand into her big leather bag and felt the butt of the pistol.

There is something I learned and cannot forget. It is this. When you shoot someone at close range the pressure on the trigger, the noise of the report, and the sight of the hole where the bullet has gone in come together in a deadly micro-second.

Judith stood at the far end of the table and felt the ringing the shot had left in her ears die away into complete silence. If Fergus gave a shout as he raised a hand in an instinctive, ineffectual attempt to parry the bullet she had not heard it, any more than she had heard the noise of his fall that carried a chair backwards on to the floor at the other end of the table. What she was aware of was the silence in which she stood and listened intently. All she heard was the sound of water dripping from a tap in the kitchen where Fergus had been about to make coffee, the noise – very far off and subdued – of a car starting up, solemn music filtering through from some distant radio. She could not see Fergus. The table concealed him. She slipped the safety catch forward, feeling the unexpected warmth of the metal, and dropped the pistol into her bag. She did not move from where she stood and listened.

It seemed impossible that there was no sound, no alarm, no police siren, no hammering at the door, no windows flung open in amazement, surmise and fear. But she was not afraid – merely tense, alert. Her breathing was fast and shallow but she dominated it and inhaled deeply to slow its pace. She looked round. Nothing had changed in the room, except that the man who had held her prisoner here and in her life was lying dead. She slung her big leather bag over her shoulder and walked towards the door. She had not taken more than a couple of steps before her foot struck the empty shell where it lay ejected, bright, shining, still hot to the touch. She dropped it into her bag beside the pistol. The door was not locked. She opened it and stepped into the thin sunlight of the November morning and walked down towards the noise of traffic on a main road.

To her surprise people were walking along on the pavement, stopping to look in a shop window, to buy a newspaper from a kiosk where a poster announced the grave state of the Caudillo, taking children by the hand across a wide road to the park beyond, where they could join in innocent and noisy games, waiting at a stop for a bus, hailing a taxi as she herself did and gave the address in the distant suburb where the streets bore colonial place-names. She would, she reckoned, have more than enough money to pay the fare. She sat far back in the corner of the rear seat. She had an odd, hallucinatory sense of awareness but no fear.

Soon they had left the broad avenidas behind them and beyond the old periphery were entering the zone where factories and gas works, warehouses and bus depots gave way at last to blocks of buildings in a waste of sand and bare asphalt. She had enough to pay the driver, who drove off without any apparent curiosity about his fare or what might have brought her to this address. The name was clear enough by the bell. Menendez. Who? asked Pilar. A friend, said Judith and hoped Pilar might recognize her voice, respond and not remain suspiciously barricaded in the flat. There was a click and the door opened. The lift was slow and noisy. On the landing there was Pilar.

Without a word she led the way into the flat. When she was in the safety of the kitchen Judith said: 'I –' but could go no further. Her mouth was dry but that was not what made her inarticulate. 'I –' she began again and stopped, stood there with her arms wrapped round her chest beneath her breasts, hugging herself and swaying a little, so that Pilar came over and steadied her, offered her a cup of hot milk. 'I,' said Judith for the third time and began to shake uncontrollably. Her teeth chattered. She felt suddenly cold. Then the tears came, silently at first but soon accompanied by a low cry that made Pilar take her in her arms and try to hush her.

Setting Judith down in a chair she heated the milk and coaxed her to drink it. Before the cup was empty she held out a couple of small white pills. '*Toma,*' she said firmly. Judith took the pills with shaking fingers and swallowed them down. Then she allowed herself to be led to the bedroom where Pilar sat her on the bed, took off her shoes, lifted her legs up on to the mattress and drew a blanket over her.

The sleep into which she plunged was dark and dreamless,

leaden. It lasted so long that when she woke it was already dark. She threw off the blanket and dizzy and sick made her way to the kitchen, where Pilar sat in front of the television. The news was just ending. The announcer was funereal. As Pilar turned off the set a point of light imploded on the screen. 'Well,' said Pilar 'they tried. The bomb went off all right, but the Minister escaped. One of them was blown up in the car. What happened to your friend? They rang this morning to know where you were. I said I didn't know. But what about him?' Judith heard herself say: 'I shot him.' Pilar was silent for a moment then she rose and put her arms round Judith. 'Then we must think,' she said.

The woman who came through the dark to fetch her was younger than Pilar, dark-haired, with an olive complexion. 'This,' said Pilar, 'is Juanita. She'll look after you.' They walked in silence, keeping in the shadow of the flats until they reached an older building with a shuttered shop-front. Juanita opened a door and they found themselves in what in the dark seemed to be a store-room smelling of fruit, of garlic and onions, of earth, of vegetables. At the end of a long corridor Juanita at last turned on a light. In a Spanish that Judith found difficult to follow she apologized for the poor state of the room they had entered, with its television set, its big double bed with the icon of the Sacred Heart at the head. She offered coffee, a glass of wine, of sherry, a *fino*. Her face had the same mask-like quality as Pilar's. They had worked together, Pilar and her, she explained. Pilar had always been a good friend, ready to stand up for their rights, to argue with Señora Concepcion over her percentage, to fight off the men who tried to persuade *las chicas* that they needed protection. If you were in trouble you went to Pilar, who was as strong as her name. Any friend of Pilar's was a friend of hers. She didn't know what it was all about. And didn't want to know. It was none of her business. Anyway there were times when the less a person knew the better. But here Judith would be safe until the morning.

It was in the night that a doctor, having removed the drip from the great man's arm, waited by the bedside till the pulse gave up its slow flickering and the breath rattled and died in the open mouth. As he left the room he nodded to a couple of nuns who had been sitting outside in the corridor of the clinic, their hands clasped and the beads of the rosary run between their fingers. As they rose, their beads swung down at their side. Then quietly they moved in to perform the mysteries which would prepare the great man, the statesman, the tyrant, for his last public appearance. Embalmed, he would be laid out in his parade uniform, its high gorget thick with gold braid, the cuffs broad and braided, the hands white-gloved, over his right shoulder a broad sash and on his left breast his most cherished order. So the photographer saw him and recorded the sharp nose with its cavernous nostrils and the half-open mouth that revealed a missing tooth. In the newspaper offices it would be added to those the editors had had ready for days: one, for example, of a young man, dark-haired, booted and spurred, with his legionary's cloak thrown over one shoulder, binoculars in hand, and at his side an old Moroccan, bearded, subservient, both of them wrapped against the cold of the mountains; one of a middle-aged man, smiling, self-satisfied, his right hand raised in salute, walking at the side of the Fuehrer, basking in the great tyrant's success and power; one of the same man grown fat and double-chinned embracing the President of the United States, smiling with satisfaction at this recognition of the importance of his dictatorial regime to the 'free world' in its fight against his old enemy, Bolshevism. By that time it was morning.

Pilar arrived in a hired car driven, she said conspiratorially, by a good friend of hers. Judith's suitcase, she said, was in the boot. She hadn't bothered about the rest of the stuff. She was wearing an old fur coat, scuffed at the wrists, a little tight for her, smelling of naphtha, and a dark scarf to cover her head. Juanita and Judith kissed and the car drove off through the quiet streets – like All Saints or Corpus Christi, said Pilar. Maybe he was dead at last. At the airport there seemed to be more police and Guardia Civil than usual. Pilar did not get out of the car. 'Someone came last night,' she said. 'He said the man in the car was your *compañero*.' 'But I –' Judith began but Pilar laid a hand on her lips. 'I know,' she said, 'and so do they.' She hugged Judith and kissed her. 'Be brave,' she said. 'It will be difficult – but be brave.' Judith stood for a minute or two on the pavement. She could still smell on her a mixture of mothballs and Pilar's heavy perfume. The driver got in. Pilar leaned forward and waved. The car drove off. As she picked up her suitcase and carried it into the entrance hall, Judith was nervously aware of the Guardia Civil patrolling the building in pairs.

She was ridiculously early for check-in but elected to go through immigration right away. The man in the glass cage turned her passport to and fro, glanced down at something – some list of names and passport numbers – beneath the top of his desk. He stamped a page and then indifferently, without a word, returned the document. The stamp said 20.11.75. Out on the stand men busied themselves round the British Airways plane in a slow deliberate way. In the cockpit window she could see the face of the pilot. An airhostess appeared briefly and inspected the steps leading up to the plane door. Judith was aware that her hands were moist with perspiration. She felt in her big leather bag for a tissue and found one, used it and screwed it into a ball. The bag was lighter now. Pilar had taken back the handgun and the bullets. The minutes dragged on. There was about the

150

place a feeling of tension which brought her nerves to a taut pitch.

Slowly the departure lounge began to fill with businessmen, with Spanish students bound for language schools in Britain, nervous and tearful, turning to wave through the glass at parents and boyfriends, with expatriates from the south with their tans and dark blazers and regimental crests on the breast pocket, their wives blue-rinsed with large, ornate sun-glasses and sun-dried skins.

The businessmen spoke quietly together. Two of them sitting beside her swapped rumours about the death of the great man and speculated on the succession, the role of the Army, the power of the party of which he had been head, the part the prince of royal blood might play. Judith felt that unless a voice told them to board very soon, she would be unable to control the scream that throbbed in her throat. The voice came at last. She mustn't rush, she said to herself, she must take her time. Inside the plane an air-hostess smiled brightly, automatically. Judith settled in her place. The plane was half empty. She had a row to herself and a window seat. As the plane gained height the horizon tilted and settled again. She looked down and wondered what lay beneath her. What were those hills called? What valley was that? The Valley of the Fallen or the valley of the Jarama? But she was too exhausted to peer any longer. The plane climbed slowly. Cloud obscured the peninsula, its battlefields and graves. Soon the plane seemed to hang suspended above a white, gently shifting sea. Judith was seized by deep, uncontrollable grief. She made no sound but the tears ran down her cheeks and she felt them salty on her lips. There were only crumpled tissues to staunch the flow. A hand touched her shoulder.

'Are you all right?' asked the air-hostess, genuinely concerned, handing her a couple of fresh tissues.

'I'm not sure,' said Judith.

'Can I get you anything? Water? An aspirin?'
Judith shook her head.
'Thank you,' she said, 'but I don't think it would help.'